# *14 Shorts....*

## *by*

## Dick Wild

**Grosvenor House
Publishing Limited**

This book is published by
Grosvenor House Publishing Ltd
28-30 High Street, Guildford, Surrey, GU1 3HY.
www.grosvenorhousepublishing.co.uk

A CIP record for this book
is available from the British Library

ISBN 978-1-78148-791-4

# Contents

# 14 Shorts....

Foreword: A collection of short, simple (occasionally not so 'sweet') stories, written in a range of styles and drawn from a range of situations, aimed at anyone with an eye for a simple tale and without the need to be too uplifted by the things they read.

Dick Wild.

# Lizards And People

A man had been sitting at a bar for some twenty minutes – an ageing, rickety old place of pine: pine walls, pine roof, pine tables – each wobbling in sympathy with the rickety chairs at their sides. The bar itself was little more than jumble of bottles, tumblers, fags, ornaments and just about any accoutrement that you never know who might ask for at some point in time. The air was heavy – thick layers of cigarette fog stirring round a lack-lustre fan, hot, sticky aromas of bubbling fat drifting from a cooking-area somewhere out back. A tinny speaker, hanging from a corner by a spider thread, contorted Elton John to a discordant buzz, more synonymous with home-spun eastern tunes than any accomplished Western studio operation.

The man sipped his beer and read his book. As it happened, the couple on the next table were also English – late thirties, neatly dressed in lightweight evening gear – a well groomed couple, a little out-of-place in such surroundings, as in truth, was he. In the spirit of national comradeship, they'd invited him to join them at their table. It was his customary practice to decline such invitations, but such extenuating circumstances as he found himself in, prompted him – this once – to compromise his principles.

The pair made space at the small table which, much to the husband's irritation, wobbled repeatedly as they organised the glasses, cigarettes and ash tray to appropriate places.
'You'd think they'd stick some blue-tac or something under them for Christ's sake.' Close to exasperation, he made a last-ditch effort to resolve the problem with a folded serviette.

1

'Why don't you ask at the bar dear? They seem to sell just about everything else,' said his wife, dismissing the complaint – and her husband – with a sideways flick of her head and swift exhalation of cigarette smoke over her left shoulder.

Inevitably perhaps, the conversation began with the circumstances that had brought them to the village. Their 'guest' explained the predicament that he had found himself in: arriving by bus, hoping for an easily negotiable return to the port, where he was based in a hotel some forty miles down the river. In his naivety, or maybe ignorance, he had overlooked the vagaries of buses, or more accurately their timetables, and advice had dissuaded him from taking lifts from strangers and certainly from hitching, as either could as likely lead to robbery and even murder, as to any given point on a map. Consequently, he was to all intents and purposes, marooned.

His meeting with these two could certainly be seen then, as a stroke of good fortune. They'd been given the use of a barge, owned by a Malaysian working colleague of hers. It was moored at a quiet spot only a few miles from the port where he was staying. They'd flown over from London and were in the process of familiarising themselves with the craft by barging leisurely up and down the river, stopping off at wherever took their fancy, usually a village that offered a café or hopefully a restaurant meal and a bar for the evening. Tomorrow they were continuing south towards the mooring to consider their options from then on, so obviously they could give him a lift. He would have to bed down on deck but that wouldn't be a problem in this climate and they had at least one spare sleeping bag below deck. The fact remained he had very little choice, short of walking forty miles or so, or waiting possibly days for a bus. He accepted the offer.

The 'pleasures' of meeting people on holiday had always eluded him: plodding through the tiresome details of who they are, where they're from, what they like, what they don't like – when the fact remains, you're barely interested. But there are times when one is obliged to play-the-game and this, it seemed, was such a time.

As they'd invited him to join them, it was fitting that he should be invited to tell-them-about-himself-first. He struggled through the desultory details of his job, making a number of impromptu readjustments in the hope of avoiding the tedium of interrogation that was apt to follow on these occasions.

'Well that's interesting,' said the husband. 'As long as you're happy with what you're doing. That's the main thing.'

He took his turn to reveal his own line of work: in finance, liaising with representatives of foreign companies – hedge-funding, asset-stripping and insurance investments. It was good money – he certainly couldn't complain – but he wasn't one to 'let the grass grow under his feet' so-to-speak and he already had half an eye on a possible move into longer-term investment, possibly in Europe and hopefully in The United States.

It called for another beer, his wife managing to catch the waiter's eye and he arrived shortly after bearing wine, beer and a large whisky, which in this bar was particularly large, swilling around in the glass like a basin of amber wine. With drinks delivered and a few moments taken to reduce the glasses' contents, they moved dutifully on to her line of work.

He listened as she talked about her job in London, so close to where he actually lived and worked, and in his own line of work too. In different circumstances he might have pursued it a little, but this was hardly the time or place. She confessed to feeling no real enthusiasm for the job. It was what she did – it was okay – she coped and got by one way or the other.

It ended with the collective raising of glasses to lips. She took a long drink and placed the glass on the table as her husband followed her example, taking at least two sizeable glugs of his whisky.

The conversation shifted to lizards.

'Beautiful creatures,' announced her husband taking a sidelong glance at his wife.

'Wretched things,' she responded, pointedly refusing to rise to the bait. 'I hate them. They're all over the place. They get on the boat, in the cabin.' She shivered visibly, as if expecting one to prove the point by rearing its head from behind her wine glass at any moment.

Her husband settled more comfortably in the slightly rickety chair.

'One of my wife's hang-ups I'm afraid. I keep telling her they're perfectly harmless but she won't buy it.'

She was quick to react to what was evidently a familiar routine.

'That's not the point. I'm not afraid of them. I just don't like them – that long sneaky body, those quick darting little movements. And then the stillness, when they stand stock still – just waiting for something to happen.....'

'To attack you dear....' said her husband, the grin broadening in time with a shift to a more convivial posture, the table wobbling a little under his movements.

'They don't have any conscious control over their actions. They're animals, or reptiles I suppose to be accurate. They act on instinct. You've just got to remember that they're far more scared of us than we are of them....well mostly!'

The tone was markedly more patronising than playful. His wife's response was one of restrained anger at a naughty child.

'I've told you I'm not afraid. That's not the point. I'm not talking about that. Come on.....finish your drink?'

Her husband grinned a perceived victory and obligingly downed the remainder of the whisky in a swift gulp.

His wife looked away, sucking cigarette smoke into her hollowed cheeks.

'I'm going to order more drinks,' she said, exhaling the smoke directly into her husband's line of vision. 'And I'm going to get you a double, just to shut you up.'

She raised her hand in the direction of the bar, the lizards, for the time being at least, forgotten.

Instead, they discussed the weather and the debilitating affects of its humidity, the food, difficulties with communication – the pitfalls of being foreigners in a strange land, until the clock on the wall above the bar indicated the onset of a new day.

It was shortly after one-o-clock, with enough beer, wine and whisky safely stowed away, that the three made their way through the pine door into the stiflingly still air of the night.

A small path, dimly illuminated by bulbs hanging from wires, drew them away from the shacks and sheds and down towards the river – appearing at first as little more than a series of ghostly streaks half-hidden behind twisted vines and impossibly huge trees towering above them to the tune of a thousand crickets. It took a while for their eyes to adapt and they ventured slow-stepped, taking particular care – hand holding – almost feeling their way in the dark like blind creatures.

'Tell me if there's any bloody lizards,' said the wife, stumbling over a small clump of rocks near the water's edge.

'Don't worry dear, they're all on the boat waiting for you,' replied her husband with a grin.

'Fuck off,' said his wife. She wasn't grinning.

It was quite a walk to the barge. The path continued to wind through the cluttered undergrowth that shone in a silvery metallic sheen under the moon - full and rounded in the star-dotted sky. There was an eerie beauty, but dangers lurked under the river's dazzling surface.

'It might make a pretty picture but this river's one of the most dangerous in these parts. Fall in and you've got no chance – unless you get out pretty damned quick,' said the husband, feeling his way tentatively along the vines at the water's edge.

The barge had been left in darkness. Access was by a small step ladder hung over the side. The husband led the way, feeling along the top edge of the boat, aided by moonlight but wary of his whisky-induced movements as he stepped with extra caution over the rim. The others followed, taking equal care and pausing at every foothold to plan the next in advance.

Once on the boat, they stood for a moment, gaining the confidence to balance on the undulating surface. A guide rail led them to the cabin entrance where they visibly winced against the yellow glow as a lamp was switched on.

He stayed in the cabin only briefly before making his way outside with a sleeping-bag to familiarise himself with the deck surface, testing the width and the gentle rhythm of the boat's movements. That done, he seated himself on the bench that ran the full length of one side and leant over the river, taking in the lapping sounds and the night calls of the forest beyond.

He pulled his rucksack and the sleeping bag to his side and manoeuvred each into place. He didn't expect to sleep. Instead he sat and stared across the water where the soft movements of the river-bank provided such sharp contrast to the smoky confines of the bar they had left. For a while he was vaguely aware of the murmur of voices, until the light went out and the voices waned to leave the boat in darkness and silence.

He stretched out on the seat beneath the glittering display of stars, easing himself into the gentle rhythm of the river: a light soothing rhythm that came close to lulling him into temporary sleep – when he was suddenly aware of movement much closer to home.

He raised his head from the makeshift pillow. Ahead of him were three small lizards, each no more than two or three inches long, observing him through tiny pin-prick eyes. He could just about make out their wiry shapes and tiny protruding legs. He had an urge to say something, to strike up some brief communication, but resisted the temptation and settled instead to watching their tiny jerking movements, until a few moments later, one of them made a sudden bolt in the direction of the cabin door. His eye followed it briefly and then returned to the bank on the opposite side of the river.

Seconds later, a hollow crack from the cabin sent the remaining creatures scurrying for sanctuary at the far end of the boat.

It could only be a gunshot. A sudden jolt grabbed the pit of his stomach. He rose, feeling for the rail, his legs bent and crooked, stiff as iron, sidling his way to the front of the boat, his eyes fixed on the cabin and the door to it. Once there, he stopped – his breath coming in short gasps, keeping time with his heartbeat. He stared at the door.

The woman emerged empty handed and made her way towards him. For a moment they stood face to face, and then she stroked his shoulder.

'It's okay...He's dead.....There's a bit of a mess, but he's dead!'
The silence was brief. She continued to stroke him lightly on the cheek.

'God I was so relieved when I saw you come in the bar and realised you'd made it. You obviously got up here okay then, no problems?'

'No it was alright. I got a cab like you said.'

'Good. I said that'd be best....You're sure you're okay?'

She slipped a hand over his shoulder and moved closer.

'Yeh...I'll be alright.'

'Don't worry, everything'll work out fine. We'll ditch him a few miles down river; the river'll take care of the body and we'll burn his stuff; I'll drop you off near the port and then I'll sort out what needs to be done, and I'll meet you back in London in a week or so....Okay.'

He thought so and nodded unconvincingly.

'Don't worry.'

She took his arm and they made their way together down into the cabin.

# *Twinky*

The gas station was rolling towards the end of another day. A few lights still blinked around the pumps and the light of the café shop still stretched out across the barren forecourt, toward the main road that passed by on its way to connecting with the highway toward the city. What little movement existed came mainly from stiff conifers waving and swaying in the evening breeze and the grass brushing against the line of broken fencing running the side of the road and round the station itself. There was little further activity and hadn't been following the new intersection, where most of the traffic now found its way onto the freeway passing over Le Mont to the city.

Two gas pumps stood on the station forecourt, looking in the fading light of day, like two scaling, beat up old slot machines stuck on a drive-in area of oil-stained paving with tiny growths of ragwort peeping and poking their way up through the cracks.

In the fading light, Twinky dumped two buckets at the side of the shop and shuffled his way to the door which jangled in a familiar voice as he pushed it open. The shop was a single-counter store with three or four tables, their tops perching precariously on large iron pedestals. The coffee machine sat at the end of the counter bubbling its way through the day and into the night, though whether anyone would be around to take anything from it at this hour remained to be seen. Beyond coffee, the shop had little more to offer than a handful of cookies, a couple of salami-on ryes, few cheese-tops and a box of potato chips. Behind the counter, a few lines of sodas decorated the lower shelves next to a Chicago Bears baseball pennant – one of Twinky's prized possessions, handed to him by a trucker on his way to Louisiana, and a 'Stars And Stripes' hanging from a nail next to a mirror and looking pretty bedraggled from a few decades of tobacco and cooking fat.

Two women sat at one of the tables gazing out into the increasing darkness of the station forecourt and stirring spoons into coffees that were growing more tepid and grey by the minute. Both had large puffed out faces, attempted to be made easier on the eye with coatings of make-up cream and doses of eye shadow that hung on their eyelids like tiny lug worms. Lines of scarlet lip-paint completed the picture, giving them the appearance of two old vaudeville acts, hanging on to vain hopes of a return to more theatrical times. As they stirred their coffee and mumbled conversation across the table and down into their cups, they half-heartedly raised an eye to the jangling door as Twinky made his way to the counter.

'Someone needs to get me a hose you know or some spray contraption, save me luggin' these old pails,' he said, leaning on the ice-box and dragging his feet towards the counter and the corner of the end table. 'It ain't good for a guy to be loadin' and luggin' stuff when his back ain't playing right and his hips are all but shot to pieces.'

As he reached the counter he took a firm hold of the corner and tried to find some relief stretching himself up to his full height – which in his case wasn't particularly high – being a mere five feet four from the soles of his feet to the tip of his hair.

Nature hadn't done Twinky many favours over the years, going right back to when he was a kid finding his feet trying to walk. For some reason, the right side of his body had always had a problem keeping up with the left side whenever he stepped into motion; giving him a limping shuffling movement as if he were dragging a pile of weights or a sack of oatmeal behind him – a bearable encumbrance once the bones had re-set – but a savage burden one hot summer's day in Brooklyn, when attempting to flee a neighbouring street-gang armed with baseball bats under the elevated section of the Gowanis Expressway in Red Hook.

9

The altercation had left him with two deformed legs and a hip-socket with a busted hip and a busted socket.

Convalescence had been a lengthy business and involved a move, initiated by a sympathetic branch of the local catholic community with the aid of the social services of the Brooklyn metropolitan authority: whipping him away from further potential adolescent woe and a non-existent hooker of a mother, to the more secure climes of eastern Pennsylvania. It was a generous gesture, which, give or take the occasional hiccup from him never having been able to pick his words too wisely, had found him raised in – by comparison with his formative years – something close to a stable environment.

As he'd grown into later adolescence however, trouble had again begun to rear its head and he'd eventually found himself out of home and out of work, limping and scratching his way through a series of bum jobs and minor skirmishes with various factions of local communities, culminating in an unsavoury turn of events one winter's evening at an out-of-town drive-in near Allentown, where his predilection for speaking first and thinking later, had led to two dead bodies lying on the tarmac.

A rapid exodus to the city limits, midst threats and recriminations had followed. 'Employment' – such as it was – became an increasingly hit-and-miss affair and he pretty soon found himself adopting the life of a drifter - hawking himself around the small towns of the eastern state, until, some years later and with adulthood well and truly established in his bones, he'd finally managed to secure a stake in a gas station on the periphery of the city – a busy enough venture in the early days – but with the building of the new intersection, now pretty much left alone alongside the alfalfa fields and a few lines of conifer trees.

He stopped stretching and made his way round the back of the counter to take a bag of potato chips from one of the boxes. 'Ah quit moanin' Twinky,' said one of the women, giving the spoon a little stir and glancing at her friend Grace for support.

'Yeh, give us a break. You got a place – you got a coffee machine. You get to be nice and quiet around here. What's eatin' ya?' Grace looked down into the coffee cup and then up at the plate window where, at this hour, there was little to see but the vague movements of the conifer trees over by the roadside. She returned to her story, casting a quizzical eye over the nails on her right hand.

'So I seen Tommy coming round the corner – it was two dames, one each arm.' She slipped her finger into the loop of the coffee cup for a rare sip at its contents. 'They was coming near; he was smiling you know, all neat and Mr. Cool like he's just come up with the gold nugget in the pop-corn.'

'I'll tell you what's eatin' me.'

Twinky had stooped to take the brush from under the counter and was now shuffling across the floor to the left side where he bent down to rearrange some cans. 'I get a buck for every slice of grease I got screwing round on this floor and I'd be sittin' on a yacht down Florida with a dame and a big fat cocktail with a straw and a cherry sticking out the top. Sometimes get the feeling I got a couple of kids behind me having a bust up with a couple o' grease guns.'

He had leant down to wipe a stretch of grease that had spread from the lower part of the coffee machine and as a consequence was speaking more or less down at the floor. Not that this would necessarily make a lot of difference to how much he would get listened to. Most folks were inclined not to hold too much store in what Twinky was saying any time. For now, the two women were mostly ignoring him, just like they often did.

'Well…Tommy..I seen Tommy Nabraska some o' the time over by Wellingborough.' Grace toyed with the handle of her cup and eased her head forward, eager for nothing to be wasted between them. 'I seen him working on the building down by the back of Mullen's – you know the club next to 'Speakeasy Joes."

Twinky had leant back against the soda shelf and was busily rotating a cloth against a plate he held in his other hand.

'You know I sometimes figure when I was dumped over these

parts by the women from the Hill – you know – the nuns working up Prospect Park. I sometimes figure maybe they was paid a couple o' hundred bucks for getting me out of everyone's face. And maybe they figured they was going to get a cheap vacation over Lancaster County, sittin' there 'mongst the mules and the flowers and get to take a bathe in the Susquehanna River. Sometimes I'm sure that's the case; but that's okay. I'd like to see a nun taking a bathe in the Susquehanna River.' He popped the plate down on the counter and replaced it with another.

Grace pulled her cupped hand closer to her mouth and grimaced over her shoulder.

'Aw give it a break Twinky.' She turned to look again at the line of painted nails and moved closer to Cathy.

'And then I see Tommy leaving the place – with a girl and I swear if she ain't nothin' but a child.' She gazed hard at Cathy, who returned the look, frowning and making a little whistling noise through pursed lips.

Twinky had brought a bucket through from the annexe cupboard and was busily dunking the mop in it.

'I gotta get a floor-wash; you know – one of those machines you sit on it and it takes you round in circles doing the sweeping and the washing. You girls come back next week you gonna a find me skitting round in circles doing the sweeping like a buckin' bronco with a wasp in its ass.'

'Aw quit yer talk Twinkie.' Grace was gently stirring the residue of coffee in her cup that she held raised in one hand. 'You need to get yourself a coffee machine first that don't give you coffee all grey coloured and full of grit, 'fore you get some buckin' bronco gallivantin' you round the place.'

'Yeh,' said Cathy, pointedly pushing the cup away with an exaggerated look of disdain.

'Nothin' wrong with the coffee. Let me tell ya. Only thing wrong with the coffee is when it gets to sit there in a cup 'bout two hours on the table and don't go no place. And then I gotta take the blame 'cause there aint no more than a dime in the till when I finally get to close up. That's what's wrong with the coffee.'

The two women made a further point of sliding the cups across the table and then turned their faces back toward each other, leaning forward.

'But, this other woman…Candy. You remember Candy – I used to see her all the time, downtown sometime, wearing those neat dresses – always was one for nice colours and it was Tommy used to get 'em for her.'

'Nothing wrong with this coffee. Nothing wrong with the salami-on-rye neither, 'cept for it sittin' there on the counter too long 'n getting' stale.'

Twinky was down round the floor once again, poking the mop under the counter trying to remove a brown stain that had got a little too sticky from sitting there too long.

'Goddam grease all over the place – come here you son-of-a-bitch.' He made a final lunge with the mop and then withdrew it and doused it in the bucket. He looked over towards the table.

'How comes you girls don't eat nothin'? I got a salami-on-rye just sittin' there. You can take it for forty cents.'

Grace raised her head and glanced at the counter where a lift-top lid hid a few rolls and packets of potato chips.

'Well Tommy always gets himself money somehow,' said Cathy, 'ain't never seen anyone go short when it comes to Tommy.'

'Okay – thirty cents. Come on…thirty cents. I got two more need shifting. Let me bring 'em over for you.' Twinky abandoned the mop for a second and was making his way toward the counter.

'Aw, give it a break Twinky,' said Grace, nodding her head at the counter and taking quick glances at Cathy as she was speaking.

'You got a spare salami – stick it on the fence post round sun-up and you can use it for shooting practice.' She rolled her eyes and quietly turned her attention back to her friend.

'Stead o' firing at those two gas pumps you got standing out there doin' nothin',' said Cathy, also looking towards the counter.

Twinky had dragged himself from under the coffee machine and he reached under the flap to spread the few plates a little more evenly across the glass top.

'I don't need to be shootin' at no salami sittin' on a post,' he said, withdrawing his hand and looking across at the two women. 'I got a .38 right here – second shelf – just waiting. You won't see no-one gettin' too sassy when he knows there's a .38 sittin' here on the shelf.'

'Yeh well you just take care with that thing. We don't want to be sittin' here with no .38 bullets ripping round the place.'

'Yeh,' said Grace, winking at Cathy and looking across in the general direction of the counter, 'Don't wanna see you riding that buckin' bronco shooting a .38 off every which way.'

The women giggled and leant forward into their huddle. Twinkie returned to the mop and bucket to set about wringing one into the other and cursing a couple of grease stains he'd just noticed over by the ice-box.

'You don't argue with a .38,' he said, looking down at the bucket and dousing the mop in the water.

Twinkie had emptied the bucket and was stacking potato chip boxes out behind the ice-box. It was getting late now and one thing he could always count on, as evening made its way into night time, was his hips would be as sore as a mongoose in a bear trap and his legs'd be about ready to break into two pieces. He chucked a tray of cigarette butts in the trash box and turned to the coffee machine, reaching for a cup underneath.

From where the gas station was located – out of town, verging on the low-lying hills of Lancaster County, the night sky could be an impressive sight. The two women had left their table to take in the air for a while and for a few moments they stood outside the door in the cold draughty silence, with nothing more to see or hear than the paving flags and flurries of ragwort poking up through the cracks. Standing close, they gazed up at the stars, which littered the black dome of the sky in thick clusters of diamonds and bands of sapphires.

'Sure is pretty,' said Cathy, speaking in little more than a whisper and breathing lightly.

'Yeh,' said Grace. 'Hey Twinky.' She called over her shoulder without looking back into the shop. 'You should come and take a look here – see something beautiful for once in your life.'

Twinky placed the coffee cup on the counter and flicked the lever of the machine.

'I don't trust those stars,' he said, talking more loudly to be heard above the churning of the coffee. 'I know that soon as I'm standing out there by the pumps, one of 'em's going to turn itself into one of them shooting stars and come racing down and take my head clean off my shoulders. They say there's guys up there some place speaking English. Okay, that means they're loaded with napalm carriers and a ship-load of nuclear missiles too. I don't trust anything that just sits there cluttering up the sky – like they're waiting for something.'

He raised the cup to his lips, welcoming the hot liquid washing down his scaling throat.

'Aw, take a break Twinky,' said Grace, taking her friend's hand in her own and gazing up at the sky. For some moments neither of them said a word.

A minute or so later their attention was distracted by two closer lights. They looked across the station forecourt to watch headlights approaching in the near distance.

'Hey Twinky, you might've got yourself some custom,' said Cathy, looking over her shoulder, her eyes then returning to the car's headlights.

Twinky looked towards the door and stepped out from round the back of the counter, keeping his eyes on the road beyond the station forecourt.

For a few moments the three of them watched in silence as the headlights got brighter and the car eased its way past the conifer trees toward the start of the broken fence, where it seemed to slow for a while, as if checking whether the gas station was open or maybe, in the darkness, whether it was a gas station at all.

Grace and Cathy retreated to watch from behind the door to avoid the full glare of headlights and then returned to their seats. Twinky returned to the counter and turned a dial on the side of the coffee machine. Seconds later, the whole inside and outside of the shop was bathed in a silver-white light, causing the women to wince their heads away from the window and Twinky to glance again towards the door.

'Looks like you could be right,' said Twinky, still staring out into the nearside of the station forecourt. 'Figure he's after gas?'

'How we supposed to know?' said Cathy with a shrug.

'Maybe he just wants to hang up a while and take a break,' said Grace, looking out of the window again for any signs of movement.

The car came to a standstill and following the slamming of the door a figure emerged and made his way towards the shop. The women watched as unobtrusively as they could muster, as a man made his way through the jangling door and without hesitating, made his way to the counter. He was slim-built – maybe youngish middle-aged – with a lean overall look about him. A grey stetson reached to halfway down his forehead and a loose hunting jacket hung off his narrow shoulders. He headed straight for the counter at the opposite end from the coffee machine and reached for a stool to perch himself on. The two women watched in silence from their corner, casting quick glances to each other. Twinky waited for the man to take his place at the counter and looked over in his direction.

'You looking for gas friend?' he asked, leaning down and taking a couple of plates from a lower shelf.

The man shook his head and reached into a pocket to withdraw a packet of Winstons. Twinky waited a moment, watching the guy take the packet and with the same hand ease a cigarette into his fingers and up to his mouth. He flicked the lighter into action before replacing it in his pocket and inhaling deeply. Twinky added the two plates to the pile at the edge of the shelf. The women watched quietly from the side.

'Give me a coffee,' the man said flatly and without casting so much of a glance in Twinky's direction.

'One coffee.' Twinky turned to the machine and flicked the lever, reaching for a cup which he placed under the black spout. 'Passin' through or what?' he asked, taking a spoon and reaching for the milk jug by the potato chips. The man was too busy drawing from the cigarette to answer. He simply cocked a head in Twinky's direction and with a wave of the hand, dismissed the milk.

'You take it black huh?' Twinky slid the cup along the counter. The man took a quick glance at Twinky and reached for the cup to draw it closer.

'Sugar's right there, help yourself.' He indicated the small bowl to the left of the man, who drew once again on the cigarette and stared in front, taking the cup in his hand and raising it to his lips.

'Man of few words,' said Twinky, returning to his place and looking out across the shop with an eye on the two women, who sat watching quietly from the sidelines. Grace turned and leant forward to Cathy, who leant forward in response and said something back.

They looked again towards the counter. The man gave the coffee a few turns – the cigarette hanging limply from his lips. Twinky finished sorting the few plates on the shelf and looked up again towards the end of the counter.

'I got a couple o' cheese tops, salami-on-rye......potato chips.....' He had barely finished the line before the man raised a hand to stop him.

'Okay, okay,' said Twinky, again speaking as much to the shop, as to the man. 'Just letting you know that I got a salami-on-rye and I got a packet of potato chips. How do I know if a guy ain't eaten since yesterday?'

The man exhaled and turned an eye in Twinky's direction. And then turned again to face the shelves.

'A guy could be near starving' to death for all I know.' Twinky looked across at the women who had remained in their huddle, casting quick glances toward the counter, like two furtive schoolgirls.

'I got a salami-on-rye. I tell a guy if he's looking for a salami-on-rye, I got one...sittin' right there on the shelf.' He took a cloth from the sink and turned to wipe down the side of the coffee machine, turning an eye to the man from time to time as he did so.

'Seems you like to talk, huh,' the man said, flicking the edge of his Stetson, raising it a fraction higher on his forehead. He had kept his eyes on the shelves, occasionally catching reflections of the two women in the broken glass between the bottom two shelves.

Twinky shrugged, turning his attention to the other side of the coffee machine.

'I like to talk....I like to eat pretzels.... I like to stand here all day sticking coffee in a cup making half-beat conversation with every trucker in Pennsylvania and his goddam mom.'

The man raised the cigarette and drew deeply, resting his arms in pyramid shape on the counter. He turned to his right and flicked the ash into the ash-tray.

'Maybe you like to talk a little too much,' he said, his voice a slow, almost lazy monotone as if it pained him to be making the effort to speak. Twinky paused a second and looked up.

'Hey, cool it mister,' he said. 'What I do but speak to a customer? Don't go chuckin' the dolls out the pram fella.'

The women stared down at their cups. Neither of them spoke.

'I don't need no hassles,' said Twinky, straightening the potato chip packets and casting a look down the counter. The man raised the coffee, sipped and took another draw on the cigarette. He then looked across towards Twinky.

'Kind o' passing through anyway, since you're asking.....
Allentown's where I'm heading.' The man held his gaze on Twinky for a moment as he spoke whilst releasing the stream of smoke into the air.

Twinky hesitated a moment, as if checking out something that had just appeared on the shelf in front of him. The man had turned his face back on the shelves, his arms folded across the counter top. He drew again from the cigarette and exhaled through the side of his mouth.

Twinky drew himself up from the counter, easing the bucket to one side with his foot and glancing across at the two women, who had been exchanging further quick glances.

The man had abandoned his stool and now stood leaning against the counter with his arms folded on top. He looked again to his right and raised his Stetson a little further, revealing a thin craggy nose and narrow, almost Chinese-looking eyes. A silence fell on the shop for a few seconds as the women, who had exchanged quick nods to each other, stood to brush themselves down and make their way towards the door. Grace reached the counter and popped a closed fist over the saucer, opening her fingers to release a few coins into it. She barely looked up, but shuffled after her friend who was standing waiting at the door. 'See ya Twinky – keep the change. There ain't much of it any roads.'

She took her friend's arm and together they stepped through the jangle of the door, out into the night. Grace took a last look behind, where the man – who had cocked his head on the departing words of the women – continued to lean against the counter, his gaze seemingly fixed on the line of bottles in front of him, as Twinky leant down to wipe a cloth along one of the lower shelves.

The night air had begun to bite and both women grimaced as they pulled their coats around their shoulders and attempted to shrink into what limited warmth they offered. Arm in arm, they made their way across the paving, past the two pumps which stood like silhouetted tombstones against the pool of moonlight creeping round the side of the shed. The sky had maintained its display for Earth as the pair of them stepped over the uneven cracks and creeping ragwort.

'Sure is beautiful,' said Cathy, gazing upwards and taking a tighter hold on her friend, welcoming the soft squash of material round both their arms.

'Sure is,' said Grace, who stopped at one point and held a pointed finger up towards the sky. Her friend stood close to follow the line of her pointing and together they watched a distant light, which at first seemed to bobble and waver before easing its way gently across the sky.

They lowered their gaze, looking out across the moonlit fields where the gentle slopes of Lancaster County were by now only vaguely visible as distant black undulations on the horizon. They stopped for Cathy to reach down and remove a stone from her shoe and then they walked along the edge of darkness, peering out across the emptiness of the alfalfa fields.

They had gone no more than about thirty yards, when the unmistakeable explosion of gunfire ricocheted into the night behind them, stopping them in their tracks.

They turned instinctively and looked back toward the shop. For some moments neither of them spoke. They simply stood close, clinging to the material of each others' coats, their eyes confirming that it had definitely come from the shop. Cathy was first to break the silence.

'Figure Twinky got shot?' she said, speaking in a low voice and daring to look back towards the sole light in the darkness behind her.

'Or the guy,' said Grace, equally quietly and looking from the shop into the face of her friend. There was no movement to be seen in or around the shop, though it was difficult to see much in the darkness from where they were standing.

'Figure Twinky's hurt?' said Cathy, clinging more tightly onto her friend's arm and still staring, as if hypnotically drawn to the yellow light of the gas station.

Grace turned her eyes from the shop. 'Come on, we gotta make a move. We don't want to get caught up in no murder rap.'

Cathy hesitated. Grace turned to her friend. 'Figure a guy's gonna leave a guy to tell the tale.....whichever it is?.....Come on.'

'You figure Twinky's dead?' said Cathy, still looking back in the direction of the shop.

Her friend shrugged.

'Who knows. Come on, we need to go. We don't need to be meeting a guy who just shot a man and knows we know about it…whichever it is…We don't wanna be caught up in no murder rap.'

With a last look at the light of the shop the women turned and clinging onto each other even more tightly, made their way quickly up the road alongside the line of conifers and a broken fence, the low hum of an automobile starting up somewhere behind them.

# Keeping It InThe Family

The family had always been poor, as had their parents, their parents before them and likely their parents before them. In fact, stretching back through as many generations as could be counted, their people's circumstances had rarely risen above anything other than 'desperate' and their 'homes' – formerly hovels of mud and wattle – had graduated to little more than concoctions of corrugated tin and cardboard, the likes of which stretched more or less the length and breadth of the hot torrid lands of this particular part of the globe.

By day the family sweltered in temperatures of a hundred and twenty-plus degrees and by night they sat huddled in a tiny circle under the tin, shivering in the debilitating cold to the mother's forlorn stories of deliverance to a future paradise, which – rumour had it – promised fruit trees by waterfalls and mango as lush as water melons.

Of course, they weren't alone in their plight. Several hundred thousand – in the immediate vicinity alone – shared a similarly hopeless situation, with little prospect of improvement in the 'quality' (if that was the right word) of 'life' (if that also was the right word) in sight. What little money ever threatened to head in their direction, habitually re-routed itself to any number of International Conglomerates and World Banking Organisations, under the steady and watchful eye of a succession of politicians and leaders whose acquisition of diamond-studded palaces, fleets of limousines and private jets, bore testament to their commitment to the people.

It was one particularly hot day in August that, at the husband's bequest, the four of them seated themselves in a circle under the corrugated roof, to reflect on the bleakness of their situation, the undoubtedly bleaker prospects for the future and to make a decision.

It was agreed that the males ie. father and son (It would have to be the males, as females were forbidden from such ventures) would head to a neighbouring land, where, rumour had it, considerable fortunes were lying in wait for anyone with an entrepreneurial eye and a spirit for hard work. On their arrival, they would devote their energies to securing their slice of the 'dream', returning with it to the family as soon as possible.

Circumstances demanded that they act quickly, and so it was that the following night, the two of them bade their farewells to the wife and the young daughter Sanji and with their support and blessing, made their way past the line of dilapidated hovels which on that particular night, were illuminated almost beautifully under the early morning moon, to the path that led to the road that would eventually take them to the land of milk and honey.

As might be expected, it was an arduous journey fraught with a number of problems but their grim determination to find fortune and bring a turn-around to their circumstances drove them on. Occasionally they were able to hitch lifts in wagons, which, though invariably packed to the hilt with goats, metal drums and a range of other paraphernalia, usually had space for a limited number of travellers, albeit pressed against the sides of the truck like sardines. There were times, however, when conditions on the wagons became almost unbearable and at almost every mile it seemed another body would lilt to its side and remain so until they finally came to a stop.

Eventually, after eight days and nights of hitching lifts and schlepping foot-sore over the scorched desert, father and son reached the brow of a hill.

From the standing point just by its summit, they could look across the valley and cast their eyes across lush pastures of green and solid squares of *real* buildings, stretching before them into the distance like some scene from paradise. They allowed each other a grin and a mutual slap on the back before beginning the descent that would take them to the outer reaches of this rich and fertile land.

Back in the village, things were looking decidedly grimmer. The heat burned more ferociously than was the norm for the time of year and – banned from all public venues – the mother and daughter were reduced to scavenging from the heaps of garbage and occasional droppings of passing trucks by the light of the moon.

The fruits of their labour were scanty indeed and it would be a weary pair who, in the early hours of each morning, dragged themselves back to their hut, where they would nurse each other, and the mother would hum the plaintiff lines of an old song (quietly of course, with music having been banned for bringing pleasure) that told of a mother's lament for a son lost in battle.

As it transpired, the father and son weren't having things entirely their own way either. They were just two of a whole host of new arrivals bordering the lanes, bringing traffic to a standstill and causing considerable consternation to a number of the locals, some of whom gazed passively from their windows, whilst their more militant-minded ventured to doorways and street corners – often in groups of three, four or more – to voice their disapproval and resentment at the latest batch of newcomers. Some held placards advising..*Slingoes go home now.....No Slingoes in this house...* ['Slingoes' it seemed, was their word for the newly arriving refugees.] Gangs of burly men would shout from the pavement and congregate in bars to moan about *'Slingoes 'nickin' their jobs'* and *'smelling like their donkeys.'*

But the father and son pressed on, their lives of drudgery having, if nothing else, toughened their resolve and steeled their resistance to being too easily brow-beaten. Had they had the opportunity, they would have pointed out to the locals that far from taking work from them, their aim was to use their initiative – honed from years of hardship – to work for themselves and hopefully contribute to the community, both financially and culturally, thereby bringing benefits to all.

It was certainly an unfamiliar environment that they found themselves in. Bars and cafes lined the street. Tall glass-fronted buildings speared the sky and large blocks of fully cemented houses ran the lengths of the avenues where spruce trees had been planted in thin lines purely for show.

The pair found themselves gazing round in awe, like two children suddenly dropped in a candy factory and already, a sense of hope began to edge into the over-bearing sense of hopelessness that had all but engulfed their lives hitherto.

Alas, for the wife and daughter, there was no such air of optimism. First of their problems was being female. Being banned from public places, banned from working, banned from talking, and banned from any number of other useful aids to existence, did little to ease their lot.

But even this paled to insignificance one hot and dusty afternoon, when the rumour began to circulate the shanty camps, that their water supply – what little there was of it – was to be 're-assessed'. There were gasps of horror and a sense of disbelief amongst the people, who knew exactly what the term 're-assess' would actually prove to mean.

Confirmation arrived a few days later on the official-looking paper fliers dropped from a helicopter onto the hovels and alleys, informing them that new and unforeseen demands in 'Belair' – an estate of private villas organised in privately controlled estates, some forty miles away – necessitated the re-routing of part of the water supply from a source at an outer district near Koulembi. (The 'demands' being those of the Belair residents who, after a brief 'residents association' meeting, had agreed that a second water fountain on their estates, would save their guests the inconvenience of having to leave their quarters for refreshment.)

That night the mother sat with the daughter to consider the bleakness of their situation and the even bleaker prospects that seemed set to befall them. With even less water at their disposal, they faced little prospect than – along with several thousand other people in the area – to simply perish on some nearby rubbish tip.

The mother reached for her daughter's hand and looking steadily into her eyes, outlined the only solution available...

They must turn to relieving others of what little they could surely spare!

They would – in short – become thieves. They would journey across the flatlands by the light of the moon to the outer districts, where they would hide like hermits until the opportunity arose to take a little from those who, when all's said and done, would feel no hurt from surrendering it to avoid the pair of them dying like rats on a garbage heap.

There was silence as the daughter gazed at her mother in an expression of horror. Quite apart from the risks, hadn't God made it clear that to steal was wicked – they'd be damned to hell for eternity.

The mother hushed her child and reached across to take her other hand.

'Listen Sanji...To take a few coppers from those who have barrels of gold? To take a cup of water from those who have private pools? As opposed to dying an ignoble death in the gutter. Tell me where God lies in this conundrum? Who is about to steal *our* water? Who are the real thieves Sanji? Look around you. Can you not see that it is *men*, who – from time immemorial – have, for their own ends, sought to reduce us to desperate states of submission or leave us for dead, by spreading hate and rumours and fears of hell and damnation?' The daughter thought for a moment, desperate for an alternative course of action to avoid the proposition her mother had put forward.

'But father and Tonka. They may have found work. They may already be making plans to return with untold wealth.....'

'Tush! forget it Sanji..... Do you *really* imagine your father and brother can walk into another land and find these supposed riches with such ease?'

'But when they proposed it you agreed. You gave them your blessing.'

'Of course I did....Of course I gave them my blessing. Go on...do it...Go to try and find untold wealth.... Just don't expect it to happen that's all.'

There was a pause as the mother squeezed her daughter's hand more firmly and looked even deeper into her eyes.

'We women need to look after ourselves. It's the only future we have...Do you see what I'm saying?... Please – I need you with me Sanji. Think. Do we really deserve to die for the sake of a small bag of rice and a daily cup of water?'

The daughter thought for a moment and then amidst a wave of tears reached across and clasped her arms around her mother.

'No mother...We do not deserve to die for so little. I am with you.'

The mother let out a protracted sigh and rocked her daughter back and forth against her. This time it was her tears that spilled out onto both their shoulders.

Meanwhile, back in 'the land of milk and honey', the sense of hope, stirred on their arrival, was rapidly waning to a not-unexpected sense of frustration. After an initial few days of enquiries and searching there seemed to be little prospect of getting themselves on any kind of employment footing and they had met with nothing but the shaking of heads and at times open hostility and threats.

After yet another day's fruitless search, the weary pair sat on the steps of a building that, along with another twenty or thirty refugees, they had managed to take refuge in, and took stock of the situation. The father was despondent and about ready to abandon the venture and return to their home empty-handed.

The son, however, being more resilient and robust by nature, was not yet ready to concede defeat and the next morning, with something resembling a twinkle in his eye, he urged his father to remain in or around the building while he set off to investigate an idea that had been buzzing around in his brain since shortly after their arrival.

As requested, the father spent the morning scouring the neighbourhood's streets and the afternoon sitting in the sun with a tin held under his chin, whilst the son headed off in the opposite direction.

It was around one or two-o-clock the following morning that the son finally returned to find his father lying on the blanket in their corner of the room, almost beside himself with worry over his son's prolonged absence. He gestured to his father to step outside the room a moment.

Once outside the door and alone on the landing, he opened his palm to reveal pieces of shining silver. The father gasped and stared in disbelief. He was on the point of questioning his son, but was immediately stopped in his tracks, his son tapping his lips with his finger as an indication not to make public knowledge the turn of fortune that had come his way. The father understood but was clearly bewildered by the sudden and unexpected turn of events and it had to be said, a little uneasy; for he was only too aware of a rather impulsive and at times impetuous side to his son's nature. The son however reassured his father that it was all 'on the level' and the following day, urged him to remain in the building once again, whilst he ventured off alone, this time for maybe two or three days, in pursuit of further rewards for his efforts and initiative.

It was three days later, at about the same time in the morning – about one-thirty or maybe two-o-clock, that the son entered the room and beckoned for his father to join him out on the landing.

Together in the low light from the single hanging bulb in the hallway, the son, peered into his father's eyes and with a self-satisfied grin, opened his fingers to reveal more pieces of silver, and even a few gold coins, nestling in his palm. The father gasped and reached out to run his finger over the metal spheres as if to convince himself that they were as they seemed – real coins of unspeakable wealth. Still grinning, the son popped the coins in a pocket and proceeded to withdraw a purse from his side. Without shifting his gaze from his father's eyes, he shook the bag in front of him. The bag shuddered with gold and silver; a deep pile of, maybe seventy, eighty, a hundred or more coins, secreted in the dark recess of the cloth. Again the father gasped and with the son's permission, took hold of the purse, feeling as full a weight of disbelief as of silver and gold hanging from his hand.

Again, he was about to put the obvious question when, again, the son pressed his finger to his lips and took his father to one side.

'We cannot talk in the public haunt of men,' he said. 'Here, come to this recess and I'll explain all.'

The son led his father to a darkened corner of the hallway where the pair crouched together in the gloom.

Back in the village, the mother and daughter's plans to venture into crime were going to take some planning. The risks were high; for a woman – even taking a breath of evening air unaccompanied by a male, could lead to fifty or sixty lashes; on a bad day...maybe a dose of stoning or even hanging over on the football ground, which had been recently commandeered and renovated to full seating capacity for the purpose.

Utmost caution was essential and for their opening venture it was only once the dark clouds of night had all but brought visibility to an end, that they dared leave their shack. The lane they needed to take was a mile or so from home and they'd need to move in swift bursts from shack to shack to the path that would take them past an array of make-shift tents and cabins and the smouldering fires of the early evening.

For once, luck was on their side and they managed to reach the road and from there, by keeping a low profile, were able to walk the miles that took them to the homes of the lower-middle classes.

These were not the huge, spacious estates of Belair, for to pursue their business there would have been suicidal given the scale of security: electric fencing, machine-gun patrols, massive spike-topped walls, rabid dogs and a twenty-four hour cross-border station guard checking documentation before permitting entrance. To even consider working there would be folly and the pair had settled instead for a smaller batch of pleasant houses in a closer area known as Tamaski, which, whilst claiming strains of affluence, was far from the inaccessible fortress that was Belair.

The *modus operandi* they had devised would not involve entering premises. For even in Tamaski houses were surrounded by high spiked walls with every entrance sealed with bolt locks the size of half-bricks. The method they'd gone for was to skulk around in the bushes, waiting for a resident of the area to return after a night's entertaining – hopefully involving a heavy consumption of alcohol (banned officially, but consumed with gusto by those with the means and contacts to obtain it) – to be grabbed by the mother and held in an arm-lock on the ground whilst the daughter took the purse to remove just so much as would buy a few plates of rice, a few muffins and a few bottles of drinkable water. The purse would then be replaced in the owner's pocket and the two would make their escape into the bushes on a pre-arranged route, avoiding pursuit and subsequent capture.

It was a good plan and in theory each trip would enable them to make at least enough money to get by for the following few days, before returning to their shack as the sun would be about to appear over the mountains in the east.

There was however, an unforeseen stumbling block waiting in the wings – a lack of people to rob!

During the first week, on two occasions only had they been able to wrestle a drunkard singing songs of a dubious nature to the ground and a woman smoking a pipe. Neither had been relieved of anything more than a few coppers and it was clear that some re-thinking was required if the whole operation was to have any chance of success.

The secret to the son's success stemmed from his sharpness of eye as they had been passing through the quieter streets in the more hidden parts of town shortly after their arrival.

It had become quickly apparent to him that the traditional routes to making a few bob were almost certain to remain closed to people like him and his father and that they'd have to investigate other possibilities if they were to have any chance of securing their slice of 'the dream'.

It was during the first two or three days that he'd noticed strange comings and goings in the doorways and back streets of a certain area just behind the city centre. Further investigation had confirmed his initial suspicions.

It was in a particularly seedy, though it must be said, vibrant, part of town, that he had noticed a number of well dressed, well-heeled middle-aged men being ushered from limousines to various hidden doorways in what seemed, a particularly furtive and clandestine operation. Further investigation revealed that they were the rich ruling classes of a neighbouring land, who, having banned such outlets for sexual proclivity as brothels, cinemas or 'live acts' in their own country [such things being decadent, irreverent manifestations of an infidelic west] were obliged to fly the four hundred or so miles to this land, to avail themselves of the pleasures such outlets could undoubtedly bring to bear.

And 'avail themselves' they duly did. With an insatiable appetite and lust for 'the good life', they'd fork out oceans for a few nights in the sack with any number of the most enticingly brazen young hussies the town and its surrounding area could offer. And having sated themselves to a point of near-exhaustion, take advantage of the newly-refurbished, air-conditioned porno cinemas, to watch others 'at play'.

After little more than a day or so, with his sharpness of mind and eye and recently acquired mobile phone, the son had quickly found a route to tapping into the chain and had already secured his own line of supply which included a *'Buy one – get one free'* deal for some sixteen or seventeen pretty young things, who, for a fee, were only too ready to pander to the whims and fancies of these deeply principled, stoically religious rascals with oil in their pockets and fun-and-games on their minds. And even at that moment, he was in the process of negotiating another ten – particularly fair-skinned beauties (very much in vogue) – for special delivery in the next day or so. Of course, he had to be careful. Competition was fierce and all activities had to undertaken in a veil of mafiosa-style subterfuge. But there was money to be made...lots of it. And the son was wasting no time in organising his activities along the most lucrative lines.

The father had listened wide-eyed and opened mouthed as the son outlined his plans, disclosing each finely worked out detail that would, in the course of time, bring them untold riches. For he had no idea this kind of thing went on in these places – or any other places come to that! Of course, he was eager to hear what role he was to play in the venture, for the last thing he wanted was to be sitting around kicking his heels whilst the son was working his butt to the bone on behalf of the family. The son assured him that in time, once he had got the ball rolling, there would be a role for him – possibly as a chaperone or keeping an eye on the limousines parked in the nearby streets. But for now he must be patient and stay off the scene to allow him to get things off the ground.

Back in Tamaski, mother and daughter were struggling to make any in-roads into their venture. There just weren't the punters. The majority of the residents were reluctant to leave their houses on foot, aware as they were of the horrific crime rates publicised daily in newspapers and on the various news channels; and when forced to venture beyond their own four walls, they deliberately avoided having much money about their person. In the last week and a half they'd rolled two maids of honour and a tax collector; the fruits of their labour having blessed their stomachs with a handful of oat biscuits and another of rice. But they knew they must persevere, for one cannot expect these things to happen overnight and with a fortitude, borne out of years of hardship, they continued to take their places each and every night, behind the mulberry bushes about twenty yards from the road's edge, hoping that at any moment a peddler or late-night philanderer might appear round the corner with a little more in his purse than just a few bits of shrapnel and a bus ticket.

Back in town things were taking off....Big Time. The son certainly had a flair for the trade and each and every morning he would return with an even greater bulge in his pocket and a livelier swagger in his walk. Having had so little all his life, he was determined to make the most of having dragged himself out of the gutter, and was wasting no time in taking advantage of his new-found wealth.

After a matter of days gold chains clanked round his neck, thousand dollar watches and sparkling bracelets hung from each wrist and only the finest designer shirts and jackets hung from his shoulders. His trousers too bore only the trendiest designer labels and in keeping with the current fashion for young males with a swagger in their walk and a statement to make, were worn extremely baggy, to about halfway up his backside.

Accommodation had been a second priority and it wasn't long before they'd moved into a spanking new open-plan complex, complete with the latest kitchen range and breathtaking scenes overlooking the docks, made even more breath-taking in recent months by bulldozing a few miles of corrugated tin and cardboard junk that passed as 'homes' for a bunch of dead-beat families and an assortment of waifs, strays and down-at-heel junkies.

Every morning the son could be seen strutting his way down the road in his newly acquired rolling swagger, a mobile phone thrust to each ear to catch the low-down on his latest deals. And each night the father waited patiently, hoping to hear what part he would play in the new and exciting venture. But sadly, each night he got the same response; that it was going to take time to get things rolling and he would just have to be patient. Or at least that's what he thought he was hearing, for it was actually getting to be quite difficult for the father to make out anything the son was saying, as – in line with his new-found eye for style – he had taken to speaking in a strange parlance using a number of expressions that were at times unintelligible to the older generation such as his father.

Truth be told, it was all a bit too much for the father to take in, so sudden and unexpected had been the rise from abject poverty to unimagined wealth. And it was with more than just a tinge of frustration that he slipped yet another DVD into their latest player to while away another few hours, for he knew that he had something to offer and a contribution to make, if only he could be given the opportunity. And yet, as the days passed, the opportunity seemed to be no nearer appearing on the horizon.

Their lives followed a familiar routine: The son would leave their apartment in the early hours of each morning and return some time after midnight with a glint in his eye and bags – later to become cases – of silver and gold.

The next priority was of course a car, for forever schlepping round on foot was both inconvenient and tiring. And it wasn't going to be any old pussy car either, for apart from the demand for style, the son was looking for an appropriate manifestation of his rapidly burgeoning sexuality. The answer was the latest sports job complete with an array of fins and lights that lit the thing up like a Las Vegas cabaret act whenever he stepped on the gas or shoved on the brake.

The son was positively drooling over his new 'toy' and on his days off and at weekends, would squeeze himself into the matchbox size interior and spend hour after happy hour screeching round the streets and squealing into U turns, to head back in the direction from whence he'd come, in a brazen display of his new-found wealth and prosperity.

But for all their fun and games and lucrative business pursuits, the pair hadn't forgotten their promise to return home bearing their slice of 'the dream'. The son was in the process of tying up a few loose ends in the purchase of his latest 'live-show - peep-show' parlour and then they'd be in a position to head east to start sorting things out back on the mud-flats.

Back in Tamaski mother and daughter had been forced to re-evaluate their *modus operandi*. A 'plan B' was needed. They would turn their attention to cars; a means of forcing them to stop to enable the occupants to be robbed.

But again, there lay a number of potential difficulties. Waylaying and rolling a drunken late-night reveller was one thing, but getting into his car to set about him as he sat at the wheel whilst taking care of the passengers in the process, was quite a different proposition. They would need some means of bringing the car to a standstill and then some kind of anaesthetic to comatose the car's occupants to enable them to go about their business.

As it turned out, both proved to be more straightforward than might have been envisaged. The means of bringing cars to a standstill lay right there in front of them en-route to Tamaski – torn pieces of broken tin from the corner of their shack and nearer Tamaski, shards of broken glass that could be placed across the road to puncture the tyres of approaching cars, bringing them to a gradual standstill. There was a point not far from where they'd been operating, where the road took a number of quite sharpish bends, which – combined with the lack of street lighting – slowed cars' speeds to little more than a gentle saunter, rendering their immobility a relatively straightforward and safe procedure with little risk to life or limb.

Utilising local resources also proved to be the key to the production of the anaesthetic. It was simply a matter of gathering some of the most fetid, putrid matter off the numerous garbage piles and trenches near their shelter and on returning home mixing it with a smattering of the most pungent, polluted water that trickled down the nearby alleyways. Once canned, shaken and left for a day or two, the concoction would mature to a most noxious brew that would wreak the most pungent of gases, which – when inhaled at close quarters or taken directly into the olfactory lobes – whilst not life-threatening, would be heady enough to cause temporary blindness, hallucinations and paralysis. Of course, they had no way of knowing that – at that very moment – there was a world-wide market for such stuff just waiting in the wings to make them rich beyond their wildest dreams!

They wasted no time in setting about preparing the concoction and gathering some shards of tin and glass. That done, it was simply a matter of waiting for the fermentation process to complete before making their familiar nocturnal trek to the road that would take them to Tamaski.

Father and son, ever-mindful of their family responsibilities, loaded the car with sacks and cases of gold and set off past the glass-fronted tower blocks, new-age hyper-markets and electronic gizmo outlets to the road that would take them out of the valley and back in the direction of home.

It was of course, quite a different journey from the one that had brought them there. The car's air conditioning, tinted windows and the latest digital sound system combined to make their ride a pleasant jaunt through the broken belts of sun-dried earth and sand-hills rather than the plodding trudge on foot and in bulging trucks that had been their journey there.

And as he had already demonstrated, Tonka was no slouch when it came to driving his motor. In township after township, eyes turned in a mix of admiration, wonder and at times fear as the wheels skidded and slid round corners, the fins glistening under the summer sun, red white and blue lights flashing from each and every inch of the vehicle like scud-missiles traversing the eastern skies.

In truth, the father was a little unnerved by his son's rather reckless driving and regularly found himself clutching the seat as they roared up behind yet another truck packed with goats, rice sacks and a range of other paraphernalia, doing about ninety, before overtaking it at a ton-plus, narrowly missing mothers cradling batches of chickens and young babies – the middle finger of the son's left hand held rigid through the automatic window. The mothers would stare after them, senses of shock written across their faces. But the son was having none of it.
'What's your fuckin' shit man...I swear?' he would shout into the rear-view mirror, stepping on the gas and offering the perplexed mothers the rigid digit through the open window.

His father reminded him that there was no rush and it wouldn't hurt to drive more carefully, but the son guffawed and spat through the open window, shaking the fingers of his right hand as if he'd just trapped them in the door and advising his father to relax.
'Chill man and be checkin' the scene wot 'is 'appenin'.....'

Suffice to say, the journey back was considerably quicker than the journey there and it was toward the end of only the following day that they neared the district not far from the encampments on the flats. They would have to take a different route on their return; the dust tracks in the vicinity of the huts being nowhere near tailored to cope with the requirements of sports cars with flying fins.

It was about eleven-o-clock in the evening that the son leant with customary venom on the steering wheel to skid the vehicle temporarily away from the direction of home and onto the highway that would take them instead to the tarmac roads on the periphery of Tamaski.

The secondary fermentation process was complete and the noxious concoction securely canned and secreted in a safe place.

The moon was high and a vista of thin wispy clouds traced their way across the star-studded sky as mother and daughter emerged from their shack and with an ever-vigilant eye on the immediate vicinity, made their way down along the back-alleys and pathways to the lane, to take them to Tamaski.

They had, by now, found a more or less safe route of passage along the more exposed sections of their journey by moving in a series of short bursts and keeping slightly off the 'beaten track' in the shade of broken fences and along well-worn trenches and furrows. After a mile or two they were able to relax a little and step into a more brisk pace until they arrived at the peripheries of Tamaski, where they would take their place at the appropriate spot in readiness for their operations. Except, in the light of their change of plan, they now needed to move a little further along to a point at the end of a small series of twists and bends in the road.

Having arrived at the spot, the mother did a quick reconnoitre and beckoned to her daughter, who nodded and with an ever watchful eye, slipped over to the spot and joined her behind one of the bushes.

In the half-light of the moon, the mother reached into the cloth bag and withdrew a collection of broken shards of glass and tin and with her daughter keeping a look-out, took a final glance in each direction, before creeping out and placing the shards at strategic points across the width of the road just beyond the final bend.

She then returned without delay to the side-lining undergrowth, where the two backed off ten or fifteen yards to lie in wait behind a mulberry bush. The mother gave the canister of noxious brew an occasional shake to awaken the gases and maintain the required level of potency.

As the car raced hell-for-leather along the tarmac, reaching the outskirts of Tamaski in little more than an hour or so, the father and son discussed their immediate plans on their arrival home. They would take the family away from the mud-flats of course – possibly to a three bedroomed villa at Tamaski or maybe even a small estate in Belair. Then there would be Sanji's wedding to get sorted. Her husband-to-be was a distant cousin who earned a living selling necklaces of goat's teeth down by the riverside in Malawi and was – as Tonka put it – an ugly little geek with twisted legs from sitting in the mud too long. And he had stinky breath. Sanji of course, had never met him, but she was still young and would get used to him in time.

Tonka, of course, wouldn't be hanging around these parts for too long; time is money and he had his business to tend to and would need to be back in the city in a week or so. His father hadn't broached the subject of the business, but was by now, inwardly resigned to the fact that he would be unlikely to ever feature in his son's plans and would probably stay at home with the family and, with new-found means at his disposal, get a job as a plumber in Belair – where, the radio had claimed, work was currently available re-routing some piping – rather than return with his son to the city.

The moon shone radiantly from the star-studded sky as they turned into the tarmac road that took them up the hill on the fringes of Tamaski. With a jig in his seat and one hand beating the dashboard in time with the heavy rapping rhythms of the CD, the son bashed the gears into top to hurtle his way over the brow of the hill towards a series of turns and twists in the road.

It was the daughter, whose hearing was a little sharper than her mothers' who was first aware of an approaching car engine. She looked at her mother in an expression of anticipation and apprehension. The mother caught her gaze and sunk her head a foot or so further behind the bush.

The car was evidently approaching at some pace. Mother and daughter remained stock-still at their vantage point, their breath coming in sharp hammer-like bursts, their eyes peering vaguely through the meshes of foliage that hid them from the road.

In what seemed little more than a matter of seconds, floods of light speared the trees and the whirr of the engine increased to almost deafening velocity. Bends and twists in the road were of little concern to this driver as the vehicle swung left and right, almost like a snake with its tail on fire. The mother and daughter crouched lower and waited with an almost unbearable sense of anticipation for events to unfold.

The car's driver, of course, had no knowledge of the array of tin and glass shards that had been strategically arranged in his path and as the tyres ran over them a number of strange popping noises, followed by what seemed like mini-explosions seemed to emanate from under his feet. Such was the car's speed, there was little time to react or even be aware of the sudden swings in their line of movement, before a sudden veering to the left and a final involuntary lunge on the steering wheel, brought gasps as father and son clung to the dashboard and seat to be pitched over the edge of the road into the small dark ravine at its side.

'What's this fuckin' shit man....I swear?' was the son's closing cry, as the car nose-dived over the precipice into a trench and midst an explosion of shattering glass and crumpling metal, came to a sudden standstill.

In the stillness of the night, there was suddenly nothing to be heard except for the slight purring of a now defunct engine and little to see except a thin pall of smoke rising over the edge of the road.

The mother and daughter exchanged glances of sheer horror. Never in their wildest dreams had they envisaged such a violent conclusion from their plan and it was in a state of extreme shock that the mother led her daughter by the hand and almost dragged her to the road, where they made their way over the other side to the small ravine, where the car's fins protruded at an almost impossible forty-five degree angle from its depths. The smouldering wreckage lay still, like some ghostly vestige from a war-zone; a gentle whirring from the engine the only sound that broke the silence.

The mother urged the daughter to wait at the roadside behind a bush, as she clambered her way down the grassy bank to the car and its occupants.

With an aching heart she looked on the driver and passenger. Neither had been wearing seat-belts and such forceful contact with the dashboard and windscreen had rendered the pair of them beyond any hope of recognition, killing them almost instantly.

With a tear in her eye and truly crestfallen expression, the mother glanced round the car's interior. There was little more to be seen there, but as she cast her eyes over the rest of the car, she noticed that the accident had released the catch and that the boot flap was raised slightly from its surround. As she lifted the lid of the boot, her eyes widened and she drew her hand to her mouth in an exclamation of disbelief. Lines of bags and cases filled the space and even on initial examination, it was obvious that the bags contained money. Closer inspection confirmed it. And what money it was! A fortune beyond even her wildest dreams.

For some moments she examined the bags, slipping a few of the gold coins through her fingers. But then in a quick return to the moment, she withdrew her hand and made her way round to check the passenger side of the car. The passenger was clearly dead. From the appearance of the two she surmised they were a middle-aged and younger business partnership, presumably on a return from some lucrative business venture. The younger man's clothes and jewellery being clear evidence of their wealth and standing in the corporate world.

For a second she contemplated abandoning the whole scene and the sacks of gold, to make her way home with Sanji to re-evaluate their whole situation; for never in her wildest dreams had she foreseen such a tragic result from their night's work.

But then she thought again, and asked herself what was to be gained by such an impulsive act. For what would then happen to the money? It would fall into the hands of some corrupt local politicians or financiers, to be used in yet another dubious development that would serve only to make theirs, and others like them's lives even more miserable. Why should such men gain from what after all they had little hand in? But she knew that she must move quickly.

It took some time to lift the sacks and cases of coins to the ground and the mother was about to summon her daughter to come and help her lift them to a temporary hiding place behind a roadside bush, when she looked back for a last look in the car, just to confirm that both passenger and driver were indeed dead. It didn't take long. There could be no doubt about it, most of their faces and heads had been squashed to unrecognisable pulp; they were dead. And for a second, she had a fleeting thought of the sadness they were about to wreak on a family sitting somewhere in wait for the return of their 'loved ones' before she looked up in the direction of her daughter and called her over, warning her not to look into the car, for she would certainly find the scene of carnage too distressing. The daughter gasped in amazement when her eyes fell on the lines of sacks and cases. But there was no time to stand around admiring their booty. They needed to move fast, for it was possible that other vehicles may soon be passing by whose occupants may well take more than just a passing interest in a recently nose-dived sports car with flying fins.

With heavy hearts but burgeoning senses of excitement, they took the sacks one by one to a hidden spot behind some mulberry bushes. They need not worry too much about the car and its occupants. In these parts the police rarely bothered to investigate traffic accidents – particularly when it was apparent that the driver had simply been driving too fast, lost control and as a consequence, plummeted into a ditch. They had of course removed most of the shards of glass and tin from the road to avoid drawing unwanted attention to the actual cause of the crash. The police would be unlikely to examine the car itself too closely.

As if in some kind of strange dream, the mother and daughter sat behind a bush well hidden from the road and some way from the accident. They couldn't afford to be hanging around and would soon set off on their way through the forested area toward Tamaski itself. The daughter was at first shocked when her mother had said they would be heading in that direction and wouldn't be returning to their shack, for despite their new-found wealth, what about her father and brother? What was to become of them should they return home, with or without, the product of their work? The mother took her daughter's arm to relieve her troubled mind.

'Tush..Sanji..Forget your father and Tonka. How long has it been since they left? Do you really imagine that after all this time they will be returning bearing sacks of gold. And... I would have told you this earlier, but thought it best not to....

*If* father and Tonka were to come by any wealth to speak of, there is only *one way* that it could be acquired in the kind of place to which they headed. And it is a way that has no place in our hearts and no part to play in we women's lives. Do you understand what I'm saying?'

The daughter thought briefly and then nodded knowingly into her mother's eyes.

'Yes mother. I understand.'

With a smile the daughter took her mother's hand and together they reached down for the first bags of gold and turned from the bushes to head, on this occasion, towards Tamaski rather than from it.

# The Landlord

Joe Mason pushed the door to, turned the key and turned slowly into the room. He waited a moment, giving himself opportunity to steady himself from the stairs, and then shuffled across to the small surface by the sink where he stood to regain his breath after the effort of the stairs. That done, he slipped a small canvas holdall off his shoulder, down his arm and placed it on the surface next to the tea-bag tin and packet of sugar. It had been particularly quiet round the shops – silence always seeming more evident on cold mornings such as this with the sky nothing more than a shroud of washed-out grey. And the silence seemed to have followed him, hovering over the broken flags of the pavement, drifting past the hedgerows and creeping through the door and into the house. Nothing stirred. He loosened the string on the bag – it was a good bag – simple and reliable, a nicely sewn piece of canvas, a little frayed at the seams after all these years and slightly open to daylight in the tips of the corners, but it still had its strap sewn tightly to its surface, and it served him well. He withdrew a tin of baked beans, a tin of potatoes and a double roll of toilet paper from the bag and placed them on the counter and then turned to take the kettle and hold it under the cold water spout. The tap was dripping; it always seemed to have been dripping.

He turned back into the space of the room and made for the wooden armed chair that stood underneath the picture. The picture was the single feature of decoration in the room. It was of an old boat moored on a beach – maybe somewhere on the Sussex or Suffolk coast. A figure in long rubber leggings was leaning nonchalantly against the brow of the boat. The sky was grey and a seagull was perched on the front mast. He rarely looked at the picture.

Supporting himself on the arms he eased himself into the chair. Mobility had taken to creaking a little in the joints of late, bringing an urge to drag his feet rather than make the effort of proper steps – it was a sign of laziness and he was aware it was something he must guard against; he knew he mustn't allow himself to drift into a coma of laziness; sitting rather than walking, lying on the bed rather than getting up on his feet and thinking. It was too easy to drift into idle habits.

He lay against the soft cushion of the chair back, rises and falls in his chest settling into a kind of rhythm. He would get up to put the put the tea-bag in the cup in a minute. He just needed to rest his feet, which had also taken a tendency to ache recently, probably in protest at too much walking up and down the pavement. But he liked to walk the pavement in the morning or early afternoon; it awarded the satisfaction of activity and he liked Morpeth Road, only briefly, not too far; just past the lights of the furniture shop and the bric a brac of the Chinese trinket place and past the book shop and the bank and maybe Tuesdays, Fridays popping into the small café on the corner of Willow Street. They knew him behind the counter there. The girl smiled and brought hot tea to his table and a biscuit for free.

He turned – preparing himself to make the effort to get to his feet to put the tea-bag in the cup; no call for being lazy or becoming idle. Having risen from his chair he stood momentarily upright: like an old soldier marking time, bringing his limbs back into play before making his way across the room to the counter.

It was as he was dunking the tea-bag to get the liquid to the desired shade of brown that he heard the distant clasp of the door a few storeys below. He made little of it. There were often comings and goings; it could be the couple on the second floor – Turks, Greeks or whatever or maybe the black guy with the kid. Two Poles or Kosovans or whatever they were at the end of the landing. He dumped the tea-bag in the side bin before too many brown spots dripped onto the counter and reached for the teaspoon still crusted with tea and sugar from last time. As he spooned the sugar and added a tilt of milk and gave it a stir, he was aware of steps out on the corridor.

The steps suddenly stopped, and the next thing, four sharp knocks resounded through the room like a hammer. He turned instantly.

'Who's that?' A further knock rang through the room. It was hard to imagine who it could be. Why would anyone be knocking on his door? He rarely had anyone knocking at his door like this. You need to be wary in these situations.

'Wait.....Who is it?' he bent his ear to the wood, waiting for a response.

'It's me, Rana Shalack. Don't worry. Open the door.'

Joe grunted and reached down to the door lock. Mr. Shalack was the landlord or owner or whatever it was. He was never quite sure how landlords and owners and agencies quite fitted into the picture. He had only ever seen Mr. Shalack in person on a handful of occasions.

He opened the door to a tall dark figure only vaguely decipherable in the gloom of the landing. He shuffled to one side to let him enter. He was youngish - thirties plus, clad to razor-sharp precision: sharp black trousers and a black waistcoat only semi-concealed under the canopies of a flowing black coat which was worn open to drift to somewhere round the points of his ankles. Only the finest cut would suffice, from coat, trousers and jacket to the thickly gelled quiffs of tarred-black hair and seasoned layer of chin-stubble that gave the impression of a chin left lying overnight in a vat of iron-filings. A thin silver chain laced a few black hairs in the space opened at the neck.

He stopped a moment in the frame of the light and extended a hand – the hand of courtesy on meeting one of his tenants. Joe took the hand and stepped aside to allow him further entry.

The visitor made his way toward the centre of the room, where he paused, breathing deeply, taking some satisfaction at finding himself at the heart of one of his properties.

'So Joseph, how are you? It's good to see you again.' The clipped tone didn't appear to demand any immediate response. Before the opportunity for one arose he had seated himself in the second chair to the right of a small two-draw sideboard. Joe watched him take a seat and then made his own way to the chair opposite.

'I get by,' said Joe, easing himself back into place nestled into the cushion of his seat. His own speech, though soft in tone, had an eloquence and precision that seemed largely at odds with his generally down-beat appearance. He raised his head to his visitor, curious as to why he should have descended upon him in this fashion. The landlord awarded himself some moments to take stock of his surroundings, reminding himself of the decor and internal furnishings of one of his more 'basic – lower end of the market' properties. He turned back to Joe.

'I was just passing,' he said. 'I was in the area so I thought I'd pay a visit on one of my more long-standing and valued tenants.' He looked away again.

The words, bright and breezy enough, did little to lessen Joe's sense of unease. Joe said nothing but watched him rise and make his way across the centre of the room, where he turned with a semi-swirl of his coat to face him. He reached into his pocket and withdrew a packet of cigarettes.

'Okay if I smoke?' He was already tapping one of the contents into his fingers.

'If you like. I don't have an ash-tray.'

'It's okay. I'll use the sink. I'll rinse the sink after, don't worry.'

'It's your sink,' said Joe.

There was a silence as the cigarette was lit and the first plumes of smoke released into the room. The landlord continued his surveillance, checking that all was in order. He took a long satisfying draw on the cigarette.

'So is everything in the room okay? Is the property catering adequately for your every need?' He looked at Joe, a searching look as if to gauge what lurked in the minds behind dusty old tank-tops and stained and baggy trousers. For a moment there was no reply. Joe twiddled his fingers and did his own quick reconnoitre of his rudimentary surroundings.

'As I say Mr. Shalack ....I get by.'

'Call me Rana. I don't mind. It's my name.'

The landlord leant towards the sink and flicked the ash. He eyed the broken linoleum floor and its scarred patches of hardened glue, a stark reminder of the Spartan conditions of some of his people's existences.

'So, it's potatoes and beans today then Joseph,' he said, observing the tins standing by the sugar.

'And a bit of mince,' said Joe, looking over his shoulder to make himself heard. 'I've a little bit of mince left in the fridge from yesterday.' He turned his eyes toward the tv set's blank screen. Rana stood by the sink, popped the ash again and turned to face the centre of the room.

'Problem with the tap?' he asked, observing the droplets popping onto the chrome base of the sink.

'Just dripping, that's all,' said Joe, looking up again in Rana's direction. 'It's always dripped. I've turned the tap as tight as I can manage but it doesn't make any difference. It still drips; gets on my nerves sometimes..night times..on and on, drip drip drip....like someone tapping a drum.'

Rana looked down, giving the offending appliance a hefty wrench and watching a temporary lull in the dripping.

'I'll get it fixed,' he said. 'I'll have someone up Thursday.'

Leaning against the shelf he turned his eye back into the room.

'So apart from the sink, any other complaints? What about heating? It must get pretty cold up here in winter, draught creeping up the stairs. You keeping warm?'

Joe's eyes shifted uneasily to and from his landlord. He could see no reason for Mr. Shalack being here, unless it was to bring news. And 'news' from men like Mr. Shalack – property men – landlords – meant changes: places being bought, sold, people being moved on, new people appearing. Rana was quick to spot the unease in his tenant's eyes.

'I'm not going to do you any harm Joseph; you know that. I told you, I was passing by and I had a mind to pop in and check that everything was okay. That's my job. I own the property. I'm your landlord.'

Joe turned his eye towards the small two-barred electric fire and nodded in its direction.

'It does get cold sometimes. But I use the fire there…Both bars sometimes. I have no choice. The wind creeps up the stairs and under the floorboards. Some nights you get ice at the bottom of the windows near the panes.'

Rana looked briefly in the direction of the window and then at the small metal dome next to the skirting board with its two coiled burners, one sagging and one slightly distended.

'Hardly adequate. And expensive. Ideally you'd have central-heating like everywhere these days but it isn't really feasible. I'll get you a better fire, more modern – radiator type, transmits heat by a system of closely synchronised fans.'

Joe stared at the fire and then looked up.

'Do you want a cup of tea?' he asked.

'No…don't trouble yourself Joseph – I'm strictly a coffee man. Don't you worry yourself.'

Rana turned to where the tap had resumed its dripping and the cold air outside had brought patches of misty condensation in the lower quarters of the window. He cast his eyes out through the window over the rooftops and a length of street visible beyond the trees. He hunched himself on his elbows, a concerted effort to distance himself from the words that followed.

'I'm moving Joseph. Selling up and moving.'

Joe looked up from his seat.

'Moving where?'

Rana hesitated, his attention held for the moment on the misty horizons of West London.

'California,' he said, giving it a few seconds consideration. 'Sunshine State.'

He turned once more into the room and tried giving the tap an extra twist. He abandoned it and turned his attention instead to two small knobs on the front of the *Belling* cooker.

'The details are mostly worked out.'

Joe brushed a fist against his nostrils and looked up.

'When you going then?' he asked.

'Don't know yet...Depends,' said Rana. 'Few things need sorting.'

He finally abandoned the kitchen area and made his way back to the room, resuming his seat a few feet from Joe.

'So....you're okay then, that's good.' Rana tapped his fingers in a regular beat on the arms of the chair. Joe held his gaze in the vague direction of the tv screen, his fingers scratching blindly against a palm in his lap. He looked up.

'So what about me Mr. Shalack? Where do I stand? Am I a sitting-tenant or something of that sort?'

'Call me Rana.'

'I don't know what happens when properties such as this get sold.'

Rana followed Joe's example and placed his own hands firmly in his lap.

'We'll see Joseph, we'll see. There's a few things need sorting yet.'

He reached to his pocket and withdrew a small notebook and pen, in the manner of a tv detective about to take notes from a witness.

'So there's the tap.' He scribbled quickly on the paper. 'And...we'll look into the heating.' He stopped his annotation and slipped pen and notebook into his pocket.

He leant back in his seat and looked at Joe. A long, searching look.

'San Diego's the place. San Diego, California. You heard of San Diego Joseph?'

Joe shrugged.

'Heard of it yes.....Once or twice.'

'Beautiful – long curving bay – golden beaches – girls. Beautiful.' He paused, turning the beautiful images over in his mind. Joe looked up from his lap.

'So you going to sell the place?' he said, twisting the fingers of one hand into the palm of the other, scratching nervously at the skin.

Again, Rana struggled to offer any immediate answer. He rose from his chair and made his way over to the window, where he turned swiftly, the coat tails floating temporarily at his side like two pterodactyl wings. He flicked a hand; a gesture for Joe to join him.

'Come over here a minute Joseph.'

Joe hesitated, reluctant to make the effort of leaving his chair.

'Come on, over here. Don't worry. I'm not going to push you out of the window, just come here.' Joe continued to resist the effort of getting out of his seat for no apparent reason, unaccustomed as he was to taking orders from absentee landlords.

He eventually got himself to his feet and stood for a moment for the circulation to stir to take him to the window.

'Look.'

Rana had his eyes fixed out through the window, somewhere over the western expanses of the city. Joe arrived by his side and followed his landlord's gaze over the rooftops and distant skyline.

'What?' said Joe.

'What do you see Joseph?' Rana seemed to have his gaze fixed on some point out on the distant horizon. Joe leant forward slightly for a closer view but could see nothing but rooftops and an expanse of flat empty sky.

'Can't see anything,' he said, looking left and then right and then left again. Not even signs of aircraft pitching their final descents into Heathrow.

'That's not strictly true Joseph. You can see something,' said Rana, in the manner of a schoolteacher overseeing a pupil's lacklustre attempt at a chemistry experiment. Joe looked again, but tiring at the apparent waste of energy, turned his attention back towards the centre of the room.

'Ain't nothing there,' he said.

'Exactly,' said Rana, turning with him, an air of resignation levelled in the direction of the great outdoors.

'Nothing......Grey rooftops, a few stunted trees and a grey sky......As you so aptly put it, nothing.'

He stopped and turned away from the glass, leaning against the window-sill, his eye sinking to four dustbins and the broken pathway beyond them.

'I'm thirty two years old Joseph. I have five properties. You're sitting in one of them, one's in Acton and there are a few in Turnham Green and another in Earls Court. And there could be more to come, why not? Property is where money is made.'

He turned once more towards the window.

'Do you realise Joseph, that you and thousands like you are sitting in nothing but ugly little piles of grey piggy banks?'

'Well I know there's money in property, always been that way,' said Joe.

'But I'm going to tell you something Joseph.' Rana tapped his hands decisively against the sill – an indication to take note of something worth hearing. Though Joe's attention remained – for the moment at least – firmly fixed in the palm of his hand with little urge to unravel what might lie behind his words. This was his house – his property. He could say anything he liked. Rana remained unmoved, his attention focused entirely on the top of Joe's bowed, rapidly balding head. Turning again to the window, an arm swept majestically above the threadbare carpet.

'Picture it Joseph. It's seventy, eighty degrees in San Diego. You leave downtown – travelling along the Pacific Highway – long lines of palm trees swaying in the sunny breeze. After about four miles you leave the highway. You pass an intersection and about quarter of a mile up on the left hand side there's a neat little place set in its own private lawns.'

He stopped, allowing a thin smile to break across his dark features. 'It's a beautiful place.' Joe shifted slightly, easing a foot towards a dark spot he had noticed on the carpet.

'It's fitness centre Joseph. A fully equipped state-of-the-art fitness centre.'

Joe tapped a foot tentatively against the tiny grey patch.

'Is that where you're going then?' he asked.

'That's right,' said Rana, taking Joe's wriggling foot movements as a signal for his next line.

'But...it isn't quite complete....there's just one missing link....' The words came slower now, more deliberate. He waited for Joe to retract his foot.

'The place needs a caretaker – a watchman, 'janitor' they call it. Someone to keep an eye on things, do a bit of cleaning up, locking up at the end.' He had his eye fixed on Joe, like an angler eyeing his float in the expectation of a bite at any second. 'The missing link Joseph...is you!'

He stared at his tenant with a look of triumph, his eyes cold and steady. Joe raised a fist to the moistening rims of his nostrils and then raised his eyes in Rana's direction.

'What do you mean Mr. Shalack? I don't understand.'

Rana tapped the sill behind him.

'I think you'd make a good janitor Joseph. Keeping an eye on those rich, pampered Californians, checking the machines – making sure they're in order.' A push from the sill took him to centre-stage.

'Picture it – a spanking new – fully equipped, state-of-the-art 'Centre For Physical Recreation And Leisure' – acres of neat-cut garden and a magnificent fountain; goldfish swimming round water lilies and minutely-formed plankton. I'll fill you in on the details a little nearer the time. And before you ask – the Visa situation can be sorted; I can pull a few strings with Immigration and Naturalisation, no problem......'

He returned to the sill, where he stood, momentarily silhouetted against the flat listless sky like some great gargantuan bat, Joe's bowed head the sole object of his gaze – the wayward strands of hair straying from his dome in fine whispery feathers. A sweeping movement of the arm followed....

'Picture it Joseph...early morning down at the waterfront; a gentle mist from the great Pacific drifts over miles of golden beaches and Ocean promenade. You breathe it all in and then turn to find yourself facing the first snow-capped peaks of the Sierra Nevada Mountains...'

Joe wiped his cuff across his mouth and gazed outside where a light from the launderette hung in the mantle of cold air like a sliver of winter sunlight. He half-turned over his shoulder, his eyes fixed firmly into his landlord's face.

'I live here Mr. Shalack.'

Rana raised an acknowledging hand.

'True Joseph. But nothing is forever.'

'Would you mind telling me how I might be disposed to become a caretaker in America_____'

'*Janitor*...Joseph...not caretaker....and call me Rana...'

Rana took the opportunity to rescue himself from the window ledge and step across to settle himself into the cushion of the seat. With fingers neatly interlocked on elbows that rested comfortably on the arms of the chair, he offered a conciliatory smile, reaching for the cigarette packet in his trouser pocket. Joe turned to make his way to the rhythmic patter of droplets on the chrome basin of the sink, reaching for the tin standing at its side.

'Do you want tea?' he asked.

'Strictly a coffee man Joseph...remember.'

'Don't have any coffee.'

'Don't you worry about it.'

Rana lit the cigarette and drew heavily on its opening inhalations.

'Better try to get used to coffee Joseph. Not at all sure about the tea in Southern California.' He grinned and blew smoke in the direction of the painting on the wall.

'Whose that?' He nodded at the figure a few feet above the settee, leaning against the side of a boat. Joe shrugged and made an attempt at stemming the dripping from the tap. It made little impression.

'Dunno, some fishermen. It's your picture.'

'Really? Must be new.'

'Been here years,' said Joe, shuffling himself over to resume his place in his chair. Rana's eyes followed his tenant's movements, marking each painstaking shuffle, the thin flapping legs, the rapidly balding head with its flying wisps of hair, the bending stoop in his shoulders as he fell with a plop into his cushioned home between the chair arms – his self-contained little pit. He looked back towards the window where a frieze of water droplets from the kettle's steam ran in tiny pearls down the glass.

And with a quick glance at his watch and a single leap from the chair, was once more in the centre of the room – the coat tails flapping a closing minuet around his ankles.

'Okay Joseph...got to go now. Got a couple more people to see....few more irons in the fire, as they say.'

He cocked a final eye in the direction of the kitchen.

'It's okay....you stay right there – don't you trouble yourself, I'll see myself out.'

With a hand on the doorknob, he turned a departing eye on the figure in the chair and above him the fisherman leaning nonchalantly against his boat.

'I'll be in touch Joseph.....'

Seconds later, he was out of the door. Joe heard the steps descending to the ground-floor and the click of the outer door and moments later, a car engine disappearing into the West London traffic.

He sat for a moment, allowing his breathing to settle in slow easy rises in his chest, before he stood to make his way to the sink where he looked out over the streets and rooftops of Shepherds Bush and took the carton of milk to the fridge. He turned back to the sticky patch he'd discovered earlier. The fact was he'd been lying; he'd never even heard of San Diego. He extended a foot – it seemed like a bit of dried marmalade. Behind him, the tap resumed its dripping.

# A Small Metal Plate

One sunny day there was a man who, whilst walking towards the station and approaching a pedestrian crossing, failed to look down to the ground, and consequently, failed to observe a small metal plate protruding some two inches or so from the pavement. His foot unexpectedly struck it and he unavoidably – and with no awareness of what was actually happening – plummeted to the ground, where his face smacked against the concrete. Initial sensation was of a loud buzzing down the left side of his face and a sharp pain like a screwdriver being inserted about two inches to the left of his left eye. For a moment he remained still, as people in the vicinity flocked towards him showing considerable concern and consternation.

Concurrent conversations considered the appropriate course of action. There was unanimous agreement that it was a careless place to put such a plate, particularly as it appeared to serve no other purpose than to trip people up. And if the authorities had put it there, they were culpable. They then looked down at the man who had taken to writhing on the ground, wondering what on earth had happened. Moments later, the pain rescinded but it was agreed that the appropriate course of action would be to summon an ambulance. Typically, there were no street-police in evidence, so 'Emergency Mobile Services' were activated by one of the bystanders and some fifteen minutes later a wagon arrived. Initial examination confirmed that a visit to the hospital would be advisable and once he had been loaded into the wagon, they set off to the hospital that served that particular zone.

At the hospital they were sympathetic and angry when they heard about how he had come about his injuries. They held his head under a sharp light and probed and pushed it this way and that and then sent him for an x-ray. At radiology they photographed him from various angles and asked him what had happened. When he told them, they too rolled their eyes.

Fortunately, his injuries didn't prove to be too severe – concussion, heavy bruising and severe pain. And after minor treatment he was allowed to go home, but a period of convalescence would be required before he could return to work.

The following day as he sat in pain with his feet up in his lounge, looking in a mirror observing the bruise mature to a four or five inch mauve and green smear across the left side of his head, he took stock of the situation and decided that he would do something about it; that he would seek action, for although he was a simple man seeking little more than a quiet simple life, he was not a rich man, and still in considerable pain down the left side of his head. And – there was a principle here. Plus…it could easily have been much worse.

He surfed the phone-contact on his screen for any likely-looking numbers, eventually coming across one that looked a possibility.

He rang it and they told him to hold the line. He waited for a few minutes and then a few further minutes and then put the phone down. He picked it up and tried again and they told him to wait. After a minute something clicked and the music stopped and a voice told him to give his postal code, identity reference, name, d.o.b. and to wait a moment. He was asked what he wanted. He explained his situation. He was told to wait a moment and then asked for some details. He explained how he had been walking along when he had tripped over a metal-plate and injured himself, and that he couldn't give that any further details because it all happened very quickly. He asked if he would be entitled to compensation, but the man said that he was unable to answer that because he was from a different department. But if he wanted to go ahead and formally submit a 'claim', he could give him a number for the people to contact. He thanked him and then the man gave him a number and hung up.

He looked at the number and rang it. A voice asked him to give his personal details and asked him what he wanted. He explained how he had tripped up in the street and hurt himself. He was asked to confirm what he had actually tripped over, had it been an inanimate or an animate object. He confirmed that it had been an inanimate object. They asked him to wait a moment. It took a while because the person who would normally have dealt with this was off sick, but he eventually got through and they asked him to give some details. He explained that it would be difficult because it all happened so quickly, but he told them about the plate and they asked him whether he had evidence - whether anyone had seen what had happened. He said 'yes..a number of people'. They asked him for names or personal references, but he explained that he didn't have these details – that he hadn't been able to write them down because he'd had nothing to write with or on. They asked him if the incident had been caught on CCTV. He said he didn't know but he couldn't recall there being any camera, though he wasn't seeing straight at the time. They asked him whether the police had been involved. When he said 'no', they asked 'why?' and he said because there had been no police around at the time. They then asked him, in light of what he was saying, how he could prove the accident had actually occurred. He told them about his face but they said that under the circumstances his face was irrelevant; some people would go to the most extraordinary lengths in situations such as this. But given that it was a relatively straightforward incident, with the appropriate medical evidence he might get lucky.

The speaker pointed out that claims such as the one he was contemplating, involved the submission of documents which could either be collected in person, or forwarded in the post. He would also have to make an appointment to have the form verified and processed. He asked if he could go ahead and make an appointment, and they said they could connect him to the appropriate person – or people – if he wished to proceed with the claim. He confirmed that he wished to do this, and they connected him to someone who took his details and then gave him an appointment time, but added there was no guarantee they would see him at the time appointed. He said he could understand that and then they both rang off.

The next day he set off to collect the form from the Municipal Building. He donned on his slacks and an open-necked shirt and with a plastic bag in his left hand to put the form in, he left his flat and caught the tram to the building which was some two kilometres or so away in the next zone.

The building was a large glass-fronted affair, about twenty five to thirty storeys high with slanted sides peaking to the sky like a huge glass pyramid. Before he entered the building he stopped in front of it and gazed up at the expanses of sky and clouds reflected in the huge panes.

On entry he reported to the 'reception area' which was a long metal table with a series of intercom machines, screens and an array of other interactive devices. He spoke to the reception machine which instructed him to go to the Fifth Floor, Area Six. At Area Six he had to wait on a seat until an 'operative' was available.

It was fairly busy in Area Six with a number of families, couples and single people milling around, looking at forms and each other, whilst asking questions and looking hopefully at doors or signs pinned to walls. As he sat on his seat waiting patiently with his plastic bag in his lap, he occasionally touched the side of his face which was still extremely painful and decorated with a large purpley, yellow bruise.

After about fifteen minutes his number was announced from the speaker and he made his way to a desk.

A small man with a thin face and nose that leaned slightly to the left offered him a seat and asked him what he'd done to his face. He explained that he had tripped over a plate in the street and that that was why he was here; to pick up the form to make a claim. The man went to check which *particular* form he'd need and returned three of four minutes later waving a booklet in his hand.

'This is the one.' He took his seat and moved things aside to make space. Without looking up he explained the procedure.

'Okay, now as your claim involves physical injuries, this is the form 567–38/56-C which you have to take away and complete. Fill in all sections and sub-sections. If some sections aren't relevant put a line through them or write N/A; don't leave them blank or it will be assumed that you've overlooked them and that will delay things. Use a black ballpoint pen. If you make a mistake, cross it out and re-write the entry; don't attempt to change your first entry as this might cause confusion and delay things. If you attempt to disclose inaccurate information you could be prosecuted under the 'Municipal Services Act'. Is all that clear and do you have any questions?'

'Can I fill the form in now and then hand it in before I go?'

'No. There are people behind you in the queue and the form is approximately fourteen pages and takes some time to complete. You'd be better off doing it at home.'

So with the form safely enclosed in his plastic bag, he made his way out of the building to the tram stop to make his way home.

The form was in fact much more a booklet – as the man had implied. There were some sixteen pages all told, of purple and yellow bordered sections and sub-sections and he decided to leave it on the kitchen shelf until the following day.

The next day he woke a little earlier than usual, stroking the side of his face and yawning in an attempt to ease the pain. He put the kettle on and popped two pieces of bread in the toaster for his breakfast. Once he'd eaten, still with some difficulty and discomfort, he took the purple/yellow form to the small table in the middle of his room and switched on the small wall light. With the stipulated black pen in hand, he read through the opening advice, grasping some of it and then set about the business of completing it.

There were a number of sections on his *medical state* to be completed: childhood illnesses, skin disorders (eg. blackheads), fungal infections He confirmed that his hair and teeth were his own (except for a front crown) and could sit comfortably for more than one hour; get out of the chair independently and remain upright for more than thirty minutes. He ticked 'yes' for ability to distinguish 'light' from 'dark' and confirmed that his bowel movements were regular enough and that he was capable of urinating unaided.

There then followed other sections on his status and employment. Everything seemed to be ticking along fine. The last section was a blank page, where he was asked to describe in detail the incident upon which his claim was based. He described how he had approached the lights to cross the road and had tripped over the small metal plate in the pavement, injuring himself to the extent of requiring medical treatment at the hospital. All that remained was to enclose medical confirmation from his doctor, sign the document and put it into the big brown envelope.

The medical report from the hospital would confirm his injuries and thus help validate his claim, but it would take some time to be popped in the post due to staff shortages; but his appointment wasn't for two and a half weeks and by that time he would have everything in place to return to the Municipal Building.

On the day of his appointment he woke feeling invigorated because it was sunny and because at the end of the day he would likely be a fair bit richer. There'd been a number of similar cases on tv where victims of negligence had been awarded several thousands of pounds or more, though he didn't want to build his hopes up too much.

When it was time, he dressed in a shirt and tie and a smart pair of trousers and his black shoes that he even put a bit of polish on for the occasion. He put the brown envelope containing his form in a plastic bag and stepped out of his flat into the warm afternoon sunlight to make his way to the tram stop.

The Municipal Building looked particularly impressive that afternoon – tall and shiny against the metallic afternoon sky and he whistled to himself (though he still found it a bit uncomfortable to do so) as he made his way through the doors to the long table at the 'reception area'. Being familiar with the procedure, he headed straight to the 'reception machine' which instructed him to go to 'Eighth Floor' Area Eleven.

With plastic bag in hand he strode passed the doors and notices and arrived, via the elevator, at Area Eleven where he reported to the desk and was told to take a seat and wait. He took his place on one of the plastic seats against the wall and rested his plastic bag on his lap.

He waited as numbers were called and people responded to the call. Sometimes there was no response and then operatives appeared from doors to repeat the number using a 'haler', often with still no response. They then discussed what to do and decided to miss that number out and go onto the next. They avoided calling the peoples' names out as many of the operatives wouldn't be able to say some of the names and this would cause further confusion and delays. There was a long wait between each number and after forty five minutes he still had some way to go. But it would be worth it in the end and he had to keep reminding himself of that.

He gazed round at the notices on the walls, sometimes stroking the side of his face, and glancing round at other people until, after a while, he felt himself starting to doze.

About five minutes later he was jolted back to life, when the number announced on the machine was his. He made his way through the first door and then along the short corridor to a second door on the left. He knocked and was invited to enter.

It was quite a large room with cream coloured walls and a series of orange side lights placed at regular intervals, creating a soft almost soporific effect. There was a large white desk in the centre with a woman in her blue and grey uniform sitting behind it. She had a round, flat sort of face with indistinctive features, making her nose and mouth quite difficult to spot at first glance. A strong pair of spectacles sat on her small nostrils, looking rather like a pair of mini-binoculars.

Just behind sat a second, younger woman who looked a bit like a cat with a little round face and slightly slanted eyes. Her attention was focused on a screen to her left.

The first woman looked up and asked for his documentation while inviting him to take a seat in front of the desk. He withdrew the envelope from his plastic bag and handed it to her. She carefully withdrew the form/booklet and placed it on the table. She looked up again and commented on the bruise on the side of his head. He told her briefly about the accident. She tutted and turned to the form.

'Right. You've completed form 567-38/56-C as part of the process of submitting a claim under the 'Municipal Rights Act' and you're now presenting it for affirmation. Is this correct?'

He confirmed that this was so.

'Right, after a few routine questions, I'll examine your entries to confirm that everything is in order. You'd be amazed how many mistakes we find and under the old system we had to rectify them afterwards, which was enormously time-consuming.'

He said that he could imagine with some people that would likely be the case.

'This is Ms. White who is a junior operative and is here to observe that procedure is correctly followed and to act as witness in the event of verbal or physical assault. Now…did you complete the form yourself?'

'Yes.'

'And to the best of your knowledge, has anyone tampered with it since you completed it?'

'No.'

'Is the information you have disclosed accurate to the best of your knowledge?'

'Yes.'

'And are you related to, or do you have relations with, anyone employed in the Municipal Building, or for the Municipal Authority?'

'No.'

'Good....Now if you'll just remain seated I'll go through the form and check that everything's in order...okay?'

'Yes.'

'Good.'

She took the form and methodically eyed her way down each section, sub-section and appendage to sections and sub-sections; turning each page slowly, focusing her full attention on each entry. She occasionally made a slight humming noise, which he took as confirmation that all was well, at least so far.

The procedure took some time and he occasionally allowed his attention to wander. It had been quite a long day, and this, added to the effects of the orangey glow of the lights, soon started to make him feel quite sleepy and he felt his eyes beginning to close.

The second woman remained pre-occupied with her screen most of the time, though she occasionally looked up and there were occasions when their gazes met and he thought he could detect the faint trace of a smile, though he could of course have been imagining it. She was quite an attractive young woman with her neat, feline face and a smart flop of jet black hair hanging over her right cheek.

'Right...' announced the first woman some time later, having completed her check and having read the medical report from the hospital.

'Good. I'm pleased to announce that so far everything seems to be in order.'

He said that he was pleased to hear this but pointed out that he had been unsure of, or forgotten, some reference number they'd asked for in the first section, but she assured him that this would be clarified and recorded by the authority and not to worry about that. She moved the form to one side and leant forward on her elbows.

'Now…All that remains is for your claim to be analysed and assimilated by the appropriate authority. The hospital report has arrived and if you wait for the assimilation process to complete, you will receive the result and any accompanying compensation in Area Five – The 'Exit Area' on the ground floor, before you leave. However this does take some time and we cannot advise how long you will have to wait. It's possible that it won't take very long at all. You will be given an 'exit number' to let you know when your claim has been processed. Alternatively, you can have the results forwarded by post. Which would you prefer?'

Following previous advice he opted for the first.

'Good. Well you'll get an 'exit number' from the hatch in the wall just outside and then if you make your way to Area Five and wait there, the results of your claim will be delivered in due course. Ms. White has some brief business to attend to in Area Nine before she finishes and will escort you to the elevator. Thankyou.'

Ms. White closed down her screen and stood to leave the room. He took his plastic bag in his hand and made his way out into the corridor.

Just outside the door was a dispenser, not unlike a cash dispenser. He keyed his number in and stood in silence with Ms.White waiting patiently at his side.

'It might take some time,' she said. 'Are you okay? You were looking a bit tired in the room.' She sounded a little concerned.

'Yes, I'm okay. It's been a bit of a long day, but hopefully not too long to go now,' he said, looking round to face her. 'And with a bit of luck it'll all be worth it. Mind you I could use a drink.'

'Yes, I can understand that,' she said, 'It gets so stuffy in this building. I feel like a drink nearly every day when I've finished work.'

The machine had fallen silent, and showed little indication of springing into life. There were no other people in evidence and, if nothing else, a little conversation seemed a way of passing time.

He looked into her face and she looked into his. She was certainly attractive, there was no doubt about that. He coughed and shuffled his feet, not at all sure that what he wanted to say was an appropriate thing to come out with under the circumstances. He noticed that she had started looking around and then down at the ground, as if a little embarrassed or pre-occupied with other thoughts. He coughed again and deliberately diverted his attention toward the machine.

'Erm...Would you like to go out for a drink after, when you've finished work?' he asked, feeling extremely embarrassed at having asked such a question. She looked up and smiled and then looked away again.

'I can't I'm afraid,' she said. 'I'm not allowed. We're not allowed to socialise with anyone who has recently made financial gain through dealings with the authority. It's the rules. I'd lose my job.'

She looked directly at him, the sharp slanted eyes crystal-clear in the opaque corridor light.

'Well, how would they know?' he asked.

She looked at him and then at a camera poised in the top corner of the corridor.

'They'd know,' she said. 'They know about your claim and they know I've been an operative witness. It's on the file.'

For a few moments neither of them spoke. Their eyes turned to the screen of the dispensing machine waiting to see it leap into action.

'Here's your number,' she said, indicating the small ticket that had slipped out of the narrow slit in the front. He took the ticket and they turned to make their way to the elevator.

They arrived at the elevator and he pressed the button.

'Do you have far to travel to get here?' she asked. He told her about catching the tram. She nodded. A few moments later the elevator stopped at her level. She turned to face him.

'Okay then, well good luck,' she said, still smiling before turning to continue her way to the end of the corridor.

'Thanks,' he said, as the doors closed.

Exit Area Five was a large square foyer with huge exit doors to the outside in one wall. An array of dispensers of various sizes and hatches were built into the front wall with lines of blue and grey chairs facing them. He sensed that he'd have some time to wait before finding out how much he was going to get, but it would be better than relying on the vagaries of the postal system. There were a number of other people there but plenty of chairs available should he wish to sit down.

To kill a bit of time he had a walk round the walls, looking at some of the pictures and posters on display. On one wall were pictures of old buildings from the past. One was called a 'town hall' which it said underneath was a bit like a much smaller version of the Municipal Building. It was a grey stone-type building with a front that looked a bit like an old country wall. By comparison with the Municipal Building it seemed tiny and he wondered how they could deal with all their business effectively in somewhere so small. It was dated from towards the end of the last century – 1996 or 8; he couldn't make out the last number too clearly.

He yawned and realised that he was beginning to feel a little drowsy again. The long day was definitely beginning to catch up on him and he decided he might as well take his seat. With his plastic bag nestling in his lap, he sat waiting and looking round at the other people in the Area – mostly young to middle-aged couples, one or two with children and an elderly man half asleep.

It was about twenty minutes later that his number rang out from the intercom and with a sense of anticipation and some trepidation he made his way to the relevant machine and took an envelope that appeared from the dispensing box.

He checked that it was his number on the front and the correct name. The white envelope was sealed. He contemplated waiting until he was outside, but decided he might as well open it now; there was a lot of space near the door. He stood by a ledge and tore open the envelope.

The document inside was a piece of folded white paper. He opened it and started reading.

Beneath all the official numbers and gobbledy-gook was the bit he was waiting for: just a few short simple phrases....

*Claim rejected ... registered as invalid...*
*Injuries due to claimant's negligence......*

*Dated.........reference ...*

He read it two, three or even four times and then folded the paper and put it back in the envelope which he popped in the plastic bag before making his way out through the doors.

The air hit him like a cricket bat and a chill wind was blowing from the east. Though it was beginning to get dark, the distant sky was thick, like peachy yoghurt, heralding a promising day to come.

He crossed the drive and made his way to the tram stop. Just before the stop was a metal litter bin. He stuffed the plastic bag in the bin and took his place in the queue to catch the tram back home. As he waited, he glanced back at the building, but all he could make out were what looked like huge expanses of grey glass. And then, a moment later, a side door opening and a number of employees emerged from the building, one of whom hesitated and then started walking towards the tram stop.

# Crosses

He awoke and glanced across in the dark at the digital clock. It said six-fifteen, which annoyed him. He was also annoyed because it was Monday. Six-fifteen on a Monday was a bad time – there wouldn't be time to doze off again. He wished it had said four-fifteen. He turned over onto his left side and imagined a few more minutes sliding away as he gazed at the partly open door of the bedroom. He closed his eyes but only temporarily. The thin light of early morning had found its way through the crack between the curtains as a reminder of a new day. When he turned over again it was six thirty. He pulled his bit of the duvet round his shoulders to grab a few more moments. His wife was lying still, facing away from him. He could see the shape of her head pressed into the squashy surround of her pillow. He finally beat the alarm by four minutes in dragging himself to seating position before venturing to the bathroom and back to dress before going to the kitchen to put the kettle on. With a bleary eye he took the bread packet from the fridge, withdrew two slices and dropped them into the toaster. Later he heard the shuffled approach of his wife as she entered the kitchen and took milk from the fridge.

They took breakfast – toast and tea – in relative silence. They'd been married for nineteen years, four months and two weeks. Indistinct voices drifted from the radio but they weren't really listening They chewed their toast and drank their tea. After that they turned things off, grabbed their bags containing what they needed for the day and made their way to the front door. After customary parting pecks on the cheeks he made for his car and she toddled off on her walk to the station. At least it wasn't raining.

The drive to work would take him about twenty five minutes. If the road works by the hospital were still in operation it would add approximately ten minutes. He'd have to wait and see. He neither liked, nor disliked driving – it was just something he did. It was convenient. As he turned the second corner from home he turned the radio on. It was one of the news programmes where people phoned in with their comments. He kept it on the same station because he couldn't be bothered changing to a different one – you had to fiddle around with a dial and buttons for a while to get anything else and then it'd probably be pop music, so he left it where it was. The Prime Minister was talking about bringing democracy to Iraq. He tried to visualise where Iraq was – he knew roughly, but once you got as far as Israel off the Mediterranean Sea all those places tended to blend together. He could picture Egypt, down there in the bottom corner. He'd been to Malta on a holiday about four years ago. It'd been really hot and he'd suffered from sunburn across his back and shoulders.

He needed to get some petrol which was a bit frustrating. There were two or three cars in the queue – but better to get it now, then it's done. The queue tended to be longer on the way home. He took his place, fourth in the queue and waited for his turn. It wasn't long before he rejoined the traffic. On the radio they were inviting people to phone up if their pets had become too fat, but they hadn't got the heart to do anything about it. He switched it off. They didn't have a cat or a dog, though they'd once kept an eye on the neighbours' cat when they'd gone to Ibiza. His wife quite liked the idea of having a cat. If anything, he'd prefer a dog. You can do more with a dog; they tend to be more outgoing.

There were road works by the hospital which caused a long queue of traffic. As a result he arrived at work about seventeen minutes later than usual. But he didn't worry, it was still fairly early. He parked his car in the staff car park next to the skip that seemed to have been there months – years even. He wondered what it was for. He couldn't see inside it, but there was a plank of wood sticking out of the top of it – that was all he could see.

The first thing he always did when he entered the building was get a cup of coffee from the machine in the hallway. He took it into the room and put it onto the table next to the computer. He sat down on the stool and switched the computer on. He was the first in the room which wasn't unusual as he liked it that way for five or ten minutes. He looked at the digital watch that his wife had bought him for Christmas. It said seven thirty eight, which was a bit later than normal, about seventeen minutes later in fact. He turned to the computer and opened the file from yesterday's listings. He had to enter data under 'Working' and 'Idle'. The data were on his left. He aligned them and dated them to make it easier. For some of it he had to switch temporarily to 'Standard Data' and 'Formulas' which was a bit of an inconvenience. There was quite a lot to do and it took him quite a long time. He took breaks in entering the data to take sips from his cup of coffee.

About ten minutes later Harold arrived. They said 'hi' and asked whether each had been delayed by the road works. Harold had been too. He thought it was disgraceful and said that in South Africa they wouldn't stand for it interrupting the traffic like that. Harold had to complete figures to send to the 'Production Department'. He'd mostly finished 'Customer' and 'Product', but had to do some entries for 'Manufacturing' and 'Human Resources'.

Soon Julie and Thomas arrived. Thomas gave Julie a lift to save them using two cars. Also because he fancied her. Using one car was a sensible idea and meant that this morning for instance, only one of their cars had been held up by the road works instead of both of them. Harold pointed out, this time mainly to Julie and Thomas, that it was a disgrace and wouldn't be tolerated in South Africa. Julie sipped the coffee from the machine and started reducing the data from yesterday's list for the quantity of cheese balls in boxes, to get it to a suitable format for storing under 'Packaging' for the 'Conway And Rankin' file.

When he'd done his updating he went through the documentation in the tray and sorted them into relevant piles – 'Capitation', 'Personnel' and 'Production Control And Modifications'. With some it wasn't absolutely clear what should go where. You could seek advice but you had to be careful – excessive seeking of advice would be frowned upon. It wasn't their data, it was yours. So mostly he made his own decisions.

The last part of the morning he had to attend a meeting downstairs. He didn't like meetings. He only went because someone from the room had to go, so it would be democratic. When he stood up to go, Julie asked him if he was going to the meeting. He said 'yes'.

It began at ten thirty seven. The trouble with meetings was that his mind tended to wander and sometimes he started to feel a bit drowsy. The room was quite small, and painted in stark sheet white – illuminated by a series of fluorescent bulbs which stretched the width of the ceiling. The chairs were padded and grey and covered in plastic. Each had a fold-down wooden flap for you to put things on. First they reviewed 'Work Sampling' procedures – there were two modifications dealing with 'Intervals'. A representative from 'Production Control' demonstrated amendments to part of a database which had superseded some elements pertaining to principles of 'Simo Charts'. He gazed up at the clock and watched the little red digital seconds turn into the red minutes and after about twenty minutes, to the next hour. A screen appeared and he realised he was starting to get hungry. Two bar charts appeared on the screen outlining 'Net Flows' and appropriate dates. There was some discussion about the dates, and the net flows. Then a colleague pointed out the advantages they'd found to suppliers in accessing the Extranet. He was wondering what he would eat for lunch and decided it would probably be mashed potato – but he wasn't sure what he'd have with it. With a promise from an executive to review some parts of the 'Database Management System', the meeting ended.

When he returned to the room they asked him how the meeting had gone. He said it had gone okay. He finished entering some data pertaining to carbohydrate levels in cheese balls, and then it was lunch.

He went down the stairs to the staff canteen. He was ready for something to eat. The canteen was large and white with a long chrome belt to push your tray along. You selected what you wanted and the staff put it on a plate for you. Julie was in the queue and was deciding what to eat.

'What are you having?' she asked.

'Mashed potatoes,' he replied.

'I don't know what to have,' she said. 'I think I'll have some fish. It looks okay.'

He chose braising steak to have with the mashed potato and some peas too. They paid and joined Thomas and Harold at one of the tables. Each table was topped in white formica supported by a huge chromed metal pedestal to prevent any wobbling.

'That looks okay,' said Thomas looking at Julie's fish.

'What have you got, chicken?' she asked.

'Yeh. It's not too bad.'

'Is that braising steak?'

'Yes...and mashed potatoes.'

When they'd eaten, they spread out a local map that Thomas had brought down from 'Resources'. They spread it out like a tablecloth so they could each see it and with their heads bowed over the sheet, they drew spider legs with their fingers, making suggestions of possible routes to avoid the road works by the hospital. Thomas thought Branscombe Way was an option. Julie wasn't sure. They considered the possibility of going by the YMCA but the trouble there was the lights. You could go via the ring road passed the brewery, but it was quite a long way out of your way. Harold pointed out that in South Africa they wouldn't be having this conversation. Maybe it was best just to go the usual way. They put the map away.

Last night's soaps had been good. In one there'd been a shooting. They discussed who they thought the culprit was. Each gave their suggestion and then backed it up with reasons. They agreed that it was tragic when things got to such a point to be settled by violence. In a different one they discussed whether Alice should get back with Tom who was a bastard. Julie said that to be fair, some men *are* bastards and there was some agreement. Though it had to be said that some women were bitches too and there was agreement with this. They discussed the words 'bastards' and 'bitches', 'bastards' for men - 'bitches' for women. Julie mentioned the worrying link with dogs. Thomas went to buy a dessert – bread and butter pudding. Harold and Julie had cheese-cake. Holidays were considered. Thomas fancied Canada – the wide open spaces – beautiful scenery. He'd always wanted to visit Quebec too – 'Viva La France!' Julie just wanted a sun-bed on a beach – somewhere really hot and chill-out for a few weeks. Harold had thought about South Africa, but had heard that it was best to go with someone who knew the place or lived there, so he might go to Scotland instead....whisky tour! Or maybe Cuba. John was thinking of a cottage in Devon – peaceful, relaxing.
The clock said one minute past one. Time to go back.

When they got back to the room he went to his place and sat down in front of the computer. He had to open a file and transfer part of it to another file and use another part of it to open a new file in preparation for further data.

As he was doing it he glanced across the room and saw Harold standing by the window gazing out. There were white blinds in front of all the windows and during the day the blinds were raised to allow daylight inside. He asked Harold if he'd seen anything interesting. Harold said he was looking at the skip which seemed to have been there for months, even years. He wondered what it was for. There didn't even seem to be much in it – all he could see was a piece of wood sticking out of the top. He also said that the skies were darkening and it looked as if it might rain soon. It would be unfortunate if it rained, but there's nothing you can do about it. He returned to his place.

After that he had to make some modifications to 'Customer Systems' and add the latest to 'Formulas'. He told the others that he had to add the latest to 'Formulas' and they groaned and offered some sympathy. Later he stopped what he was doing and looked up at the clock. It was three eighteen. Tea break. Thomas and Julie were talking privately over in the corner by Thomas's place and Harold got up to go down to get the drinks because it was his turn. They took it in turns because it made sense. He returned soon with the drinks on a tray. As usual he had tea – he nearly always had tea in the afternoon. Harold looked out of the window again and remarked that it wasn't raining, but still looked as if it might do. They hoped it wouldn't.

He spent the rest of the day with 'Formulas'. Some time later he started to watch the red minutes clocking towards the next hour to signal time to leave. They tidied up their places and made sure they didn't leave anything. They left the room – not in darkness, because the cleaners came in next and it was down to them to leave it in darkness. In the car park they said their 'goodbye's and got in their cars. It had become much darker now and he couldn't even see the plank sticking out of the skip.

The traffic was heavier on the way home. It always was though he didn't know why. On the radio they were discussing asylum seekers and what they should do about it - people phoned up and gave their views. He was glad he'd got petrol earlier because the queue at the petrol station now stretched down to the path. He smiled as he drove passed it, but he wasn't smiling when he got near the hospital. The queue stretched down to the fish and chip shop on Carlington Road. This was because of the roadworks. He had no option but to join the queue and wait. He yawned and leant back in his seat gently tapping his knee as he gazed out of the car window. He watched the beam of approaching headlights, bobbling and fierce in the darkness of early evening, feeling envy at their motion. A caller on the radio wanted to know whether these asylum seekers were economic migrants. Another thought they should be sent straight home because we've got problems of our own. Suddenly there was some movement in the queue – everyone moved forwards about thirty five yards. But then they stopped again. He sometimes wished he was in South Africa.

It was about twenty two minutes before he passed the roadworks and continued at a steady speed. As he turned into the one-way-street near his home the first drops of rain appeared on his windscreen. He was glad he'd got back before the rain really started. He didn't like driving in rain; it made everything messy. But he sometimes liked the wipers – back and forth in a steady rhythm across the windscreen. When he got home he parked his car in the driveway and checked it was locked before turning the key in his front door. He nearly always got home about forty minutes before his wife and he put the kettle on and peeled the potatoes. He sat in the chair and listened to the radio and drank his cup of coffee – he usually had coffee when he first got home at night. His wife arrived home about half an hour later and they gave each other a customary peck on the cheek. He asked her how her day had been and she said 'okay.' When she asked him he said 'not too bad'. Then they made tea.

They ate chicken pie, boiled potatoes and sweet corn and then she sat on the sofa and he sat on one of the armchairs and they watched television. Two of their favourite soaps were on. One of them was about the shooting. It ended with someone standing in the shadows holding a gun in his hand. In the other soap Alice was thinking of going round to Tom's house. His wife squirmed on the sofa and didn't want her to because Tom was a bastard. It ended with footsteps approaching Tom's door. About thirteen minutes after the soaps there was a 'situation comedy' about a couple who gave the impression of getting on each others' nerves. Afterwards his wife put the kettle on. This time he had tea.

Later there was a news programme on. There was a panel of three people and they were discussing the prime minister talking about bringing democracy to Iraq. His wife was trying to picture exactly where Iraq was. He said he wasn't sure. One person was from the government and said Iraq would be more stable and would be a better place when democracy was established. Another person said it wouldn't be easy to bring democracy to Iraq. The third person said that it was dangerous to go round the world trying to bring democracy to places like Iraq. He also added that a lot of people died every day in conflicts and we must think of their families.

Finally, about fourteen minutes later, they got up and went to the kitchen. This year's calendar was hanging in front of the previous years'. It was his wife's turn. He stood behind her and watched. She took a large black felt tip marker pen that they kept in the drawer, removed the top and drew a large cross through the day's square. She then replaced the top and put the pen down. They smiled as they looked at the pattern of crosses that they'd drawn every day since January the first. She kissed him gently on the cheek and then they turned the lights off and closed the door.

They got into bed. His wife nestled her head on her pillow. He could vaguely make out the shape of her head in the squashy surround of her pillow. He looked across in the dark at the digital clock. It said eleven thirty nine. He stretched under the duvet on his left side. About seventeen minutes later he fell asleep.

# An Essex Tale

Joe Cornley eased himself over the fence to the narrow pathway that skirted it. The breeze had swollen to a light, bristling wind, thickening the sky to the east and stirring the wild grasses and elm trees to slow rhythmic dances across the fields and cattle-marshes.

Having cleared the fence, he set himself on the path that led from the last of the boat-sheds. Satisfied that the rain would likely hold off for a while, he turned to make his way back to the shelter through the saltings and cow-parsley to a stretch close to the lane that, in the other direction, would eventually lead to the village.

It was at a point where the path came close to touching the tarmac of the road, that he was stopped by a voice; a high-pitched voice – as sharp and shrill in the afternoon as the cry of a seagull or a wounded seal-pup. It was a female voice – a young female voice at that. He looked over the brook that ran past a line of hedgerow thistle, to see a girl standing on the lane, a cycle held firmly in the grip of both hands.

He gauged her to be about sixteen; looking somewhat out-of-sorts and a little bewildered by the surroundings that she seemed to have found herself in. She had a tight grip on the cycle, and as tight an eye on the lane, as if expecting someone or something to make an appearance round the bend at any moment – unless this man, who she had spotted making his way towards her across the field, was of a mind to help her. He too glanced left and right and then at the girl standing in front of him, leaning on the cycle.

She was a nice looking girl, as far as he remembered what nice girls looked like. A thick flap of black hair covered the upper quarter of her face, which was painstakingly and meticulously presented – from the finely mascara'd eyes to thinly painted lips and the light waxen coating of fleshy powder layering her cheeks, chin and the visible portion of her forehead. She waited for the man to draw close enough to the fence before venturing to get his attention.

'A'right?' she said. The voice was light and cheery – a clear attempt to get off on the right foot.

Joe nodded, observing the girl's nervous glances. She was clearly out-of-sorts standing there alone in the middle of the lane, keeping close vigil on the bike beneath her.

'I've got a bit of a problem,' she said. It came across as much an apology as a statement of fact.

The voice was recognisably 'London' or maybe 'West Essex' - the swollen vowel sounds and foregoing of consonants clearly evident.

'I'm trying to get to the village – to find an 'otel, but I've got a puncture.' She looked dejectedly towards the lower portion of the rear wheel lying flat and lifeless against the tarmac.

'Must've 'it a stone or gone over some glass.'

Joe's eye joined her and then looked to his right in the vague direction she had indicated.

'Don't think you'll find any 'otels there,' he said.

Her face dropped.

'What, ain't there no 'otels?'

He looked again in the direction of which she was speaking He would have liked to have helped. But could only shrug.

'Not the place for 'otels. Might be a B&B or farmhouse.'

The girl stared blankly, her spirits as deflated as the tyre beneath her.

'I don't know what to do.' It was – it seemed – the final straw. She stepped uneasily from foot to foot, glancing nervously though still semi-hopefully towards the nearest turn in the lane.

Joe brushed a stubble of beard and nodded towards the offending wheel.

'Well, you ain't gonna get far on that.' An obvious enough observation, but the question was, what best to be done about it? She continued to eye the road, left, right, and left again.

He ventured a few steps closer, committed to at least giving the matter some consideration. At worst, she would have to wait for some passing vehicle, possibly some farm truck, or labourer's van. He took a glance at his watch, resolved to not wasting time dillying and dallying.

'You wanna come over this way and we'll have a look at it.' The girl hesitated, realising that the solution was largely out of her hands, but a little wary as to what he may actually have in mind. Joe was already half leaning over the fence.

'Come over 'ere and give me the back wheel.' She dutifully obliged and seconds later the bike was over the fence and with the aid of an arm, she followed it, plonking herself, a trifle unsteadily by his side.

He gave the air-less tyre a routine squeeze, whilst privately rueing the afternoon's turn-of-events; a detour over the mud-ranges or flats would have had him safely on the path to the shack by now.

He looked again at the bike which was clearly going nowhere, and at the girl standing at its side: the picture of helplessness – cunningly disguised behind the façade of eye-shadow and mascara. He sighed and leant down for a closer look at the tyre.

'Ain't you got a spare inner-tube?'

The question – an obvious one under the circumstances – prompted only the shaking of her head – further embarrassment at adding complications to proceedings.

'No, I thought there was one in the bag. But there wasn't.' Joe took a firmer grip on the bike, testing it for general manoeuvrability.

'Mind you....I wouldn't know how to put it on, with all them cogs and things.' She was looking quizzically at the strange conglomeration that was the chain-set and gear system.

He patted the saddle and lifted the machine a few times, gauging the weight. And then brought it to rest a while on the ground, awarding it a few moments further consideration. He finally raised his head and tapped the saddle a few times.

'If you come with me I might be able to 'elp you.' He already had half an eye on the clouds gathering to the east. There was little time to be wasted. The rains could be on their way. He'd made his offer. The rest was up to her. The girl continued to step uneasily, still looking left an right along the visible stretches of lane.

"Ow far's the village then?' she asked.

He shook his head.

'Too far. You won't make it.'

She raised her eye to the scene that would take her away from the road. It was a scene that did little to raise her spirits – a wild expanse of flat desolate fields, where every recognisable feature of the world she knew seemed to have been obliterated in some catastrophic Armageddon, leaving a landscape of empty wind-swept grass and ghostly-looking trees.

She shivered and returned her eye to the nearest stretch of the lane.

Joe's eyes remained fixed on the bike, prepared to bide his time a while to give her chance to consider his offer.

'I might be able to do something to patch it up – put a bit o' weatherin' on it to get you movin' again,' he said, conceding that a little more detail might not go amiss.

She caught his eye and tried to smile. Neither option cheered her much, but the prospect of being abandoned – left alone in the middle of these cold, empty fields was far from welcoming. She turned a final eye on at the barren stretch of tarmac to her left, and then turned to look at Joe.

'Okay,' she said.

He nodded and turned his attention to the charcoal-grey clouds gathering in the east.

'Come on,' he said. 'We need to get goin'.'

Without further hesitation, he started walking away from the lane, whilst the girl followed, bike-in-tow, trying to keep up with his light, measured movement along the mud-path.

His face remained tight, his gaze fixed on the woodlands and narrow pathway that took them towards the marshes beyond small thickets of trees. Little was said. At intervals he turned and waited for her and the cycle, both stumbling some distance behind him. After a while, he urged her to take the lead – to try to find her feet along the thin tracks of the path. At this point there was only one direction they could be heading.

Walking behind her, gave him the opportunity to observe her more closely; the sturdy-enough legs, quite shapely in their way – filling the levi's handsomely. And the shoes. At least she wore solid enough shoes – probably Doc Martins or one of its imitators. She had a good, steady stride – slightly pigeon-toed, emphasised by leaning into the bike, particularly on the more heavy inclines. Occasionally there was the opportunity for talk. She asked his name. He told her and asked hers. 'Tanya.' She continued – leading the way, leaning a little more confidently into the next stretch of path.

Shortly after, a small shack-like building came into view about two to three hundred yards to the east. The girl stopped, drawing Joe to a halt alongside her.

'What's that?' she asked, drawing his attention to the building she had spotted.

He stopped and looked in the direction she was pointing.

'Just an old cottage – empty now, 'as been for years. Probably some old boatman's place, maybe a yacht-skipper or an oyster-catcher's in days past. Likely just a tumble-down pile of weather-boarding now.'

The girl nodded, none much the wiser for his answer and they continued in silence.

After a while he took the bike from her. She watched him take the machine into his firmer, more controlled grasp, pushing an exaggerated show of strength against the tide of grass and mud-banking.

Shortly after, the ground changed yet again, and she found herself having to side-step turrets of soft, wet undergrowth that clung to her boots, trying to draw her into its thick magnetic grip. She lifted her feet, stepping in slow exaggerated steps, like some comic stage routine in an attempt to avoid the squelching mess gathering around her.

'Careful o' the mud,' said Joe, observing the girl's hop-stepping movements around the thick green puddles. She nodded, only half successful in following his advice.

At the top of the next ridge the pathway seemed to reform, offering welcome relief to their progress. To their left was a low-lying fence and on their right, a small trickling brook that would eventually tumble its way across the flat scrubland en-route to the sea.

About two to three hundred yards further, a small building appeared in the distance. It seemed to be a shed or an out-house of some sorts. Joe stopped.

'That's where we're heading,' he said.

Tanya cradled her eyes and followed Joe and the bike along the path.

The bike was left leaning against the wall as Joe led her to the 'living area', a small rectangular stone-basin of a room, complete with drawers, stuffed horse-hair chair and fireplace set into the stone wall like a tiny tomb. A few threadbare rugs were scattered across the floor. Through a narrow doorway, was the 'kitchen' – a conglomeration of pots and pans and strange-looking metal gadgets next to a hob built above a fire-well. Outside was a shed, a ploughed stretch of earth and a wind-cheater protection of hedge-row.

The girl shuddered in the cold light and peered back to the window in the stone wall. 'D'you live 'ere then?' she said. He nodded.

They returned to the shack, where he shifted a few fishing lines and wooden boxes from a shelf resting on two piles of stone bricks.

'Park your arse,' he said, giving the plank a perfunctory wipe. She sniffed and curled her lips at the strange, slightly musty aroma that had struck her on first entering the shack.

'What's that smell?' She followed his guiding hand to park herself on the makeshift bench.

He seemed to ignore the question and made his way to the kitchen area, where he took a pan, filled it with water and placed it on the hob, under which, a small fire of brushwood and coal was quickly ignited into a low blaze.

'Probably just the air,' he said, reappearing in the gap in the doorway. 'Or it could be the rabbits. Things are different here. You'll get used to it.'

She was seated stock-still on the wooden seat, frightened to move – afraid of disturbing the air or the strange aroma that seemed to hang in every corner of the room. He reached for a small cushion nestling in the corner and offered it to her. She took it and eased herself a little more comfortably on the bench. He returned to the kitchen, glancing back over his shoulder.

'You want tea?' he asked.

'Yes please.' She was suddenly brighter – the man had tea. It brought at least a grain of comfort.

'Sugar?'

Sugar too.

'One please.'

He brought two mugs and placed one by her side. She raised it, partly to warm her chilled hands and then held it tightly into her naval – her legs drawn under the bench. She was cold and the tea was warm and welcoming. He drank too and pushed himself up against the wall opposite, nursing the mug. He then put the mug down to turn his attention to the issue in question.

'I can try to fix the tyre. But it'll take time; I'm gonna have to get the stuff ready first and even if it works, it's gonna take time to set....I can't do it today....it wouldn't be ready in time....'

He was watching her closely, looking for a reaction. The girl sipped her tea – quietly contemplating the sense of doom the afternoon's events seemed to be drawing her into.

'You can't go back across the marshes in the dark...it's too risky.'

She hunched herself further into the bench, her fingers curled round the mug like tiny claws, her feet drawn beneath her.

The solution, it seemed, was a simple one; he took a quick drink and looked at her, a long, searching look, peering out from beneath the bushy eyebrows.

'You can stay 'ere. There's space – over there in the corner; I got some blankets and a pillow.' His voice was flat, matter-of fact – as if offering her first pick from a box of chocolates.

The girl stared into the far corner of the room, thoughts tumbling in her mind – horrible thoughts.

'I can't stay 'ere can I?....wouldn't be right.'

Joe placed the mug to his side and looked up.

'Why not?'

It was a simple enough question and to him perhaps, a simple enough issue – but to the girl it was far from simple. She hadn't, in her wildest dreams, imagined such a scenario... spending the night here. She'd imagined he would be able to fix it quickly and send her on her way. She gazed blindly at the dimmed space, crushed in the corner of the room. Maybe she could have tried to get to the village after all, someone might have passed – a lorry – maybe even a police car. You can even cycle on a flat tyre if you have to, despite what the man had said. But he'd insisted.... 'you'd better come with me.' And then, across the fields, with him behind her – that was his suggestion too; she'd been aware of him looking at her at the time.

She took another drink.

He sat, flat-backed against the wall, making no move to intervene; he'd made his offer; it was up to her – it was her bike. But for her growing sense of unease.

'You'll be alright,' he said. He stopped a moment before he continued. 'I know what you're thinking. But I won't try anything.'

She looked up – taken aback at hearing him come out with something like that, out of the blue. Their eyes met, deflecting her attention towards the door and the exit beyond it – the way back to the lane, the village and the cold empty fields. The room suddenly seemed colder, curling her more tightly into the bench, her knees drawn, feet raised slightly from the weather-beaten rug.

He remained unmoved, arch-backed against the wall, looking, in the fading light of day, like some rustic monk in the last throes of meditation – his shoulders stiff and solid, eyes pin-pointed into some vague space in the corner of the room.

She found herself watching him – mirroring his movements – her hands clutching the cracked vessel, seeking to draw reassurance from its radiating warmth. And then, seconds later, retracing her steps across the cold muddy fields – her feet plodding the empty undergrowth – his bent, almost crooked frame pushing ahead, drawing her into the bushy furrows and wet clumps of earth.

Maybe it was that that brought it home – the simple observation that, in all likelihood, he didn't really want her there any more than she wanted to be there; that it was simply circumstances, or 'fate' that had brought them together; that in some ways there was little to choose between them.

She also knew that he was right about going back; there was no way she could contemplate going back across those fields on her own, in the dark. What would happen when she got back to the lane, at such a late hour, with a punctured tyre? She looked toward the corner where he had indicated she could sleep. There wasn't much space; she'd be spending the night curled up, like a cat. She looked up.

'Alright.'

Short of greater complications – she could see no viable alternative. For a moment he seemed relieved. He stood to take a blanket from the shelf, throwing it into a pile in the corner. She watched him and went to spread it more evenly on the floor.

'Here's a pillow,' he said. She took it from him, willing herself – having made her decision – to at least take some part in proceedings.

They sat together in the stone room – about eight feet apart – him now on the horse-hair chair, her – perched on a cushion on the bench. But at least the room was warm – almost cosy – heat from the kitchen hob had quickly radiated around the space and tiny patterns of light flickered across the walls from three huge candles placed on the floor.

She was struggling with her stew. Or not so much the stew itself, as the bones – hundreds of them – she seemed to be spending all her time picking tiny shell-like bits from her lips and popping them in the tray he'd given her. It was rabbit, apparently. It had a hot, earthy kind of taste. As far as she knew, she'd never eaten rabbit, and wasn't, at first, overly keen on the idea. The last time she'd been near a rabbit it was hopping around a cage with big fluffy ears. She wasn't keen on the idea of eating things with big fluffy ears. She watched Joe, seeing how he went about it. It didn't seem to bother him and once she was halfway down the dish, she'd more or less got used to it too – apart from the bones.

There were moments of conversation. He asked what she was doing, riding around on a bike, around these parts. She explained that it was where the trains went, going east from Romford, like her mum had told her. And then a few details of home – her mother's boyfriend – squabbles, arguments – needing to get away from it. Her mum giving her the money – telling her to get away for a few days – take her sister's bike and do a bit of exploring, be a bit independent. They'd done a bit of research on the Internet. She explained how she'd changed trains at Shenfield, got off at Alth...something or other....Althorne she thought it was called. And then just started cycling – she hadn't ridden a bike for years; kept to the quiet roads and at first it had been alright, it was sunny and there wasn't much wind. She was heading for the village that her and her mother had seen on the map, but then she'd somehow got a bit lost, and then, on top of that, she'd suddenly got a puncture. He sensed a bit more 'baggage' in the bit about home – but he wasn't going to ask about that.

It was her decision to get up from the bench and take their plates out to the 'kitchen'. She wanted to do something and was glad of an opportunity to shift temporarily from her back-straining position on the bench. Joe watched her stepping her way across the floor, making no move to stop her.

The 'kitchen' was at first daunting, then just confusing – pots and pans – a couple of basins, a jumble of hooked, lever-looking things and a collection of aged crockery. And above it all, a line of what looked like butchers' knives – six bare blades of varying lengths, hanging from the wooden rack just above her head. But at least she was up and doing something. It helped her feel more relaxed.

'Can I wash up?' She looked back over her shoulder, not wanting to be seen as interfering. He was busy rolling a cigarette.

'Okay. There's washing-up liquid at the side.'

For some reason, she was surprised to hear that he had washing-up liquid.

'Fill the water basin and stick it on the stove.'

She found the water in a huge plastic container – a severed plastic tub – stuck in the corner. She scooped a pan load and lifted it, with some difficulty, to the stove.

'Now light the sticks,' he said, his attention focused on the paper rolling back and forth between his fingers.

'How do you do that?' She was looking round for some matches or a lighter.

'There's a trap – at the bottom. See it? – a small plate that slides across.' He paused a moment, giving her time to get her bearings. She found it, but wasn't sure what to do with it. It was a small metal plate fitted into the lower region of the burner. She could see the handle and how it slid back and forth, but then what?

'Now you've got to light it. There's matches on the shelf. Light the paper – you can see it stuffed near the bottom. Just set fire to it, then close the plate.'

He laid himself back in the chair, licking the paper's edge, reassured of the benefits of letting her come to terms with things of her own accord.

It was like following pre-recorded instructions. She brought a light to the screwed knots of paper, waited a moment for it to 'take' and then closed the plate. She gathered the utensils and the metal cooking basin, pulling a face at the disgusting remnants of rabbit carcass. And then later – the sublime satisfaction of swishing hot, soapy suds around the basin, the knives, spoons and the mean-looking carving knife that he had probably used to kill the rabbit.

She was nearly done and was about to tell him where she'd put a few pots and a box of some metal gadgets, when she was aware of him standing in the doorway behind her – his arm planted against the wall.

'You're doing a good job,' he said.

It was her turn to remain silent. She pointed out where she'd placed the box and left the cooking basin. He nodded.

'We'll leave the fire in the pot; helps keep the room warm. It can get cold at night with no proper heating as such. Now, how about a mug of tea?' He turned to leave her to it. It was all part of her initiation.

She lifted the pot to the hob and re-lit the fire under it.

The evening had settled into a warm, comfortable fug – the odours of cooking and burning quickly dissipating in the light breeze that wafted around the partly open door.

She too had settled herself at floor level, the blanket spread thickly and the pillow brought into play behind her, bunched against the bare stone walls. She watched the way he organised himself – pushing against the wall, resting on his haunches, head held high, staring across the room like some spaced-out druggy. She followed his example, pressing herself stiff-backed against the candle-shadows that weaved and waved across the cell-like surroundings, her eye following his craggy features slipping in and out of vision under the half-licks of light, the wild tufts of shaggy hair and dark thatch of beard, the black baggy clothes – and then the long silences; the way he seemed to avoid answering questions – almost like you weren't there, but she guessed maybe that's what happens when you live on your own in a shed in the middle of nowhere – you forget how to talk. Though later, he had talked: about the oyster farm at Mersea where he'd learned about hunting and living by the land and the sea – and then later, a boat-shed along the mudflats at Burnham – falling out with the boat's owner. And then...a woman he'd met in Burnham a few months later – much younger than him. And then – squabbles, arguments. The need to get away: to be on his own – be his own man.....She sensed there was a bit more to 'the woman' bit than he was letting on but she wasn't going to ask about that.

He told her about the shack; how he'd got it from an old wild-fowler just before he'd died and spent time doin' it up more or less from scratch. About fifteen years he'd been there.

And then she asked him something that she'd been wondering about all along, but for some reason, had been a bit nervous about asking. She asked him if he ever got lonely. At first he seemed to ignore the question – just sat back and looked up, gazing at the ceiling and then he shook his head. Soon after that, she started yawning.

The blankets were quickly in place, a pillow stuck at one end. He would be sleeping at the other end of the room on a foldaway that by day was stacked against the wall. He did a quick disappearing act, allowing her to get herself ready, though it was little more than a matter of sliding under a blanket.

Once there, she curled into a tight ball – the blanket pulled tight – her arms hunched into herself, her eyes and ears pricked, waiting for his return. She heard the fall of a clasp and a bolt being drawn. Seconds later, he was back in the doorway, where he remained a while, hovering in the empty darkness, surveying the scene. And then, with the candles already snuffed out, he made his way to the far end of the room and disappeared behind a line of boxes.

She lay still – cocooned in her blanket – lost to the distant sounds of the night: a cat-call from somewhere out beyond the marshes – the wind ghosting off the sea to fill the empty spaces beyond its walls – and then, not long after, a gentle snoring from the far side of the room.

She turned and stretched a little deeper, curling her feet against the crumpled rasp of the blanket. Of the remainder of the night, she knew nothing.

Morning filled the shack in a crisp, dazzling light. She stirred to the shuffle of feet and a humming voice, vague and tuneless.

It took some moments for the previous afternoon and evening to re-shape itself in her memory. Joe appeared, silhouetted and looking almost fearsome against the glow of sunlight.

'Morning. You want tea?'

She stepped across the floor to take her turn in the doorway. He was busy testing the knives from the rack.

'Yes please.' She yawned, trying to cast off the last vestiges of sleep.

'Well – you know what to do.'

He promptly disappeared to the shed at the end of the garden. The girl made her way to the water container and set about the business of preparing tea.

She had lit the burner and was scooping water from the tub as he reappeared in the doorway. Her mind switched to her bike and the puncture that he had promised to fix – or try to fix.

'You goin' to do the puncture?' she asked, thinking perhaps a reminder might be in order. He leant down, reaching for a stretch of polythene which he drew from a shelf under the counter.

'Done it,' he said, rising to his feet and brushing past her to get to a towel hooked on the wall. She turned to check whether she'd heard him right.

'What? You've already done it.' She looked at her watch.

He took the towel and wiped a hand and then turned to the doorway, planting the towel in a heap on the counter.

'I'll have a cup,' he said, watching her take the mugs from the side. She reached for the tea-bags and the pot of sugar.

'Did it about an hour ago,' he said. 'Should be alright, but we'll 'ave to give it a bit of time. I used some rubber-tack glue from the shed. It takes a while to dry.'

He stepped outside to unhook one of the rabbits hanging from the rack.

'Good job you 'ad a pump or we'd 've been buggered.'

He returned to the kitchen, the rabbit dangling from his right hand. He dunked it on the counter, waiting for the water to boil and the mug of tea that would follow. He watched her extinguish the smouldering wood in the burner – she was starting to get the hang of things. He noticed the make-up was still holding its own – the thin lines of mascara trailed touchingly across her eyelids.

'You must get up early then,' she said, ignoring his gaze and placing the mug at the side. He took the mug and shrugged.

'Early enough,' he said.

She was trying to guess what 'early' meant, out here in the middle of nowhere.

She took her first drink of tea.

Joe shoved the rabbit across the table, reaching for the knife he had prepared to razor-sharp precision. It was time to take her education a step further. The animal was flipped from side-to-side; a kind of hors d'oeuvre display before the dismemberment that was to follow.

'We're goin' to skin it,' he announced – her collaboration in the matter taken as read. She looked at its eyes – tiny pearls peeping up from the polythene sheet.

'It's a young doe,' he said, whipping it on its back and spreading its legs. 'Older ones, 'specially bucks can be a pain in the arse.'

He placed a wooden board on the polythene and laid the rabbit on it. For a fleeting moment she saw herself in one of her schoolgirl dreams – a vet, or vet's assistant – standing on the brink of her first exploration of a family's bunny, though there was little by way of big, fluffy ears.

'Collects the shit,' he explained, straightening the sheet and turning his attention to the knife.

She watched as he steadied the knife and then slipped it slowly and easily down the rabbit – sliding the fur off its shoulders and sides like some ritual undressing, revealing soft silky pads of glistening mauve flesh – it was almost like opening a book. He stopped and turned to his right.

'Your go.' She felt little inclination to take up the offer, but nonetheless allowed his hand to guide her through the preliminary movements.

'Just separate the skin.....that's it.' His hand remained, slowing her exploratory stabs to calmer, more measured cuts.

'Easier,' he said. 'That's it....You got it.'

He stood back, allowing her space and time to get the hang of the knife's stuttering progress towards the rear legs, her arm held rigid, her hand as tight as a vice on the wooden handle.

'That's it. You're learning.'

Her efforts commended, he eased her to one side to step in and complete the operation, this time, under her watchful eye. Next came the scissors bit and then a smaller, sharper knife to remove the legs at the joint. He indicated the sharp bones – as treacherous as needles in careless hands. Finally, the *coup de grace*: cutting round the neck and with a quick flick of the wrist, removing the head by dislocating the vertebrae.

The girl stared at the marble-eyed head, suddenly adrift in its pool of fresh crimson.

'Ugh – that's really 'orrible...That's really disgusting.' A hand drawn to her face in a theatrical gesture of dismay.

'Ain't nothin',' he said.

She stood – awe-struck – as the trail of bloodied membrane was slipped through the dilating aperture that connected the rabbit's insides to the outside until it joined the slippery pile of tongue-coloured detritus at its side. He nodded towards the corner.

At his request, she steeled herself to scoop the mess into a bucket for future disposal. He directed her to a plastic tub sitting in the corner, congratulating her; she was learning – and learning quick.

'Give it a dunkin' in the water, get 'er cleaned up.'

He watched her take the headless-carcass to the bucket – a tray held beneath to catch the red drips – and lower it into the water in slow dinking dips. A thin scum of blood and fluff floated on the water's surface. She was doing fine. Back at the board, it was her turn to complete the task.

'Watch your fingers,' he said, as the portions were finally separated down the centre with a swift cut of the knife.

Job done.

The pair stood side-by-side eyeing the hunks of rabbit spread across the board. Without further delay, Joe started collecting the utensils as Tanya turned to the plastic bowl sitting in the corner.

'Is it ready then?'

She was looking down at the tyre to check the situation.

He applied a few quick routine squeezes and stood back.

'Seems alright,' he said. 'It's had a few hours so it should hold. Best not to go too far on it.'

Tanya nodded and turned her eyes beyond the fence to her return trip across the marshlands: a stretch of wild grasses and broken trees that stumbled and shimmered into a vague silvery haze somewhere above the line of sea-walls. It was like looking out across the ends of the earth.

She turned her eye back to the shack.

Joe moved a little closer, following her eye across the fields.

'Malden's a few miles over that way.' He nodded to some vague point in the distance. 'True capital of Essex.'

She nodded acknowledgement, though its significance was largely lost on her. He fingered his pocket for his first morning tobacco, looking down to begin the rolling process, and then out again across the deathly hush of land laid bare and untouched beyond the hedge-row.

'Seems quiet now, but you imagine about a thousand years ago. The Vikings...Anlaf The Dane, riots – murder. Torching visitors....terrorising women and kids...slaughtering babies...'

He blew a few trailing wisps of tobacco from the end of the cigarette.

'That's 'orrible,' said Tanya, her face crumpling to an appropriate expression of disgust. 'We done the Vikings in Year Seven....We 'ad to draw their 'elmets.'

Joe remained head-bowed and reached for a light – brief lament for the passing of an age of true spirit and adventure.

He returned to Tanya, who had lifted the bike from the wall to do her own little check on the rear wheel. She raised her head in the vague direction of the lane.

'I'd better get going,' she said, a little more hesitant now – not quite sure whether she would be expected to find her own way back.

'You goin' already?' He followed her eyes over the fence to the point of her imminent departure.

'I think I'd better,' she said.

He stood a moment and gave the tyre a final reassuring squeeze – time enough to confirm that he had done his work – his job was done.

'You don't 'ave to,' he said, brushing dust, and a few final wisps of straw from the rubber. 'You can stay a bit longer if you like...now you're getting used to things.' He looked to his left at the wall near the door.

'That can be your rabbit..... skin it....cut it....wash it in the bucket.....all yours.'

Her eye turned to the trellis, where a second creature hung limp and bedraggled, looking – in the fresh light of day – like some long-forgotten sluice-mop.

'No, I'd better go.'

He passed his eye over the flop of black hair, the finely painted rouge and the licks of mascara paint trailed across her eyelids. And then he turned to the straggled patches of grass and broken lines of hedgerow.

Without saying a word, he went to the shack wall and lifted the forlorn-looking animal from its hanging position on the trellis to take it into the shack, returning shortly, locking the door behind him.

'I'll come with you – give you an 'and – else you'll never get the bike over the fence.'

He led the way, the girl following closely – the bike now more snugly in tow. Little was said. At intervals he stopped and waited for her. After a while he took his turn to take the bike whilst she followed close at hand. They took a detour across a few fields to get to the lane a little quicker.

Once there, he guided the bike over the fence and watched her follow it to the more familiar surface of the road. She stood by it, holding the handlebars firmly in the grip of both hands.

'Thanks for fixin' it….And lettin' me stay,' she said.

He nodded and retreated a few steps.

'If you're ever out 'ere again, give me a knock,' he said.

She nodded and raised a leg to the pedal.

Half a minute later, she was round the first bend. He waited until she'd disappeared from sight.

The wheel seemed to be holding up fine.

# The Dancer

'*Recently established company require young dancers for small-scale dance/drama production in small local theatre.. incorporating ballet and contemporary styles set to orchestral scores performed by a small local orchestra. North Paris. No 'stage' experience necessary.*'

A young girl emerged from the metro station carrying a small suitcase. She wound her way along the narrow cobbled street, past the array of patisseries, small flower and fruit shops and tiny glass-fronted cafes, stepping gingerly across the arched stones, mindful that she must – at all costs – protect her feet from stumbling or slipping on the awkward surface. She wore tight blue jeans which clung neatly to her slim willowy legs and a thick pullover which shrouded her upper body in heavy waves of wool. As the lane drew its way up yet another incline, she eased herself into a familiar rhythm, drawn fairly comfortably from her years of dancing.

On reaching the summit, she followed a path for some twenty yards and then stopped, placing the case at her feet to take a small black notebook from a tiny handbag which she had been clinging to tightly since leaving the station, warning bells of street thefts ever present in her mind. She had followed the route around the church and then up the hill, reassured that she was on the right track. She breathed again and taking the case once more in hand, continued her way across the road, past a small souvenir shop where the cobbles eventually gave way to a small park area lined by a neat row of tiny fir trees.

Finding herself unexpectedly at one of the city's most celebrated vantage points, she stopped and placed the case by her feet. She flicked her shoulder length hair, loving the soft feel of it brushing against her cheeks and neck as she eyed the scene beneath her, a patchwork of dirty greys and reds pierced by occasional streaks of silver. To her left at the edge of the park area, a pathway wound its way to the beginning of the torrent of steps which led to the narrow lines of streets and alleyways on return to the metropolis below.

As she made her descent she needed to keep her eyes peeled. She had remembered the name of the café and made a point of repeating it to herself as she had left the metro she had boarded at Gare Du Nord. Guiding herself by the rail and ever watchful to avoid slipping or tripping, she made her way down the long series of steps, taking a left by the chemist shop and then a further forty yards or so to the left turn that was *Rue De Lecarge,* sandwiched between an austere six storey building and the wall of what appeared to be a builder's yard.

She stopped about twenty yards down the street and checked again with her notebook, confirming that this was indeed the place.

It was one of any number of cafes, though being somewhat 'off the beaten track', was a little more desolate and uninviting than most of its competitors. Gaunt windows advertised a few breakfast offers, but with a lack of any real conviction and served mainly to conceal the few broken-topped formica tables and long wooden counter within. She checked the name once again, replaced the notebook, glanced left and right and made her way across the street and climbed the steps to the door.

The jangling, though wreaking havoc in the surrounding stillness, brought no response. It seemed few customers ever bought into this particular corner of the locality and there was little sign of activity in front or behind the counter.

It was a minute or so later, that – as if on cue – people finally emerged. A fat waddling woman in a mottled blue apron, heaved her way through the hanging curtain in the doorway from the kitchen area, just as – a split second later – a second jangling behind her announced the arrival of two youngish to middle aged males, one distinctly the former, the other more the latter.

The girl turned at the sound and was met by the hand of one of them – a tall lean figure dressed in a black jacket. His smooth, olive-skinned features broadened to a smile as he indicated a table over in the far corner. The man at his side was, on closer examination, considerably older. He wore a long black coat and said nothing, evidently content to let his friend or partner undertake the preliminaries.

The first man glanced across his shoulder and said something to the woman who stood waiting at the counter. The girl spoke no French and was unable to grasp any inkling of the words, but the man immediately returned his attention and smile to her, ignoring the woman who turned and set about organising some cups behind the counter.

There was a sauve, easy-going manner about the man. He smiled and in a voice that slipped easily into the velvety vowel sounds of a Frenchman's English announced his name, Jack and indicated his partner, Frederick, who he explained, was associated more with the 'publicity' side of the theatre and, he added in a hushed smile, 'spoke no English'. Frederick had already slipped into a seat behind a table and taken to reading from what looked like a menu card. In contrast to Jack, he had a roundish, quite weathered old-looking face, one that seemed happier to be kept out of the public gaze.

With the gesture of a waiter in a fancy restaurant, Jack beckoned the girl to a seat opposite Frederick at the corner table. She hovered a little unsteadily, burdened a little by the case and an air of trepidation, understandable in a young girl alone in a foreign city for the first time. Jack immediately took charge of the case. She smiled semi-apologetically and slipped into the seat. Frederick temporarily switched his gaze to her, his eyes following her into the chair until, assured that she had settled, he resumed his perusal of the menu. Jack took his place and having negotiated the girl's case into a little space by the wall, extended a hand and with a smile tapped the girl reassuringly on the arm.

'So, Helen. You're name is Helen…yes?' He spoke in the assured chaperone-style one expects of a thirty-plus French male in protective custody of a pretty young female. She confirmed it with a trace of a smile, but was finding it difficult to look too long into the man's eyes, her self-consciousness taking her gaze to the street where a small cat had curled itself by a corner lamp post.

Jack wasted no time in clarifying the situation and outlining the procedure, whilst Frederick, very much the passive onlooker, observed proceedings from behind the table.

'So….you had a good trip from London.' It was more a statement than question, delivered with the same unfaltering stare that had greeted her. She nodded and looked evasively in the direction of the street.

'Good.' He smiled and tapped the table top. 'Well, let me now give you the details. The advert in the magazine I know didn't say much, but we don't want to be spending too much money on just advertising, if you know what I mean.'

The girl nodded, prepared to look him firmly in the eye. If not always syntactically sound, his English was certainly clear and lost nothing by way of effect in its typically soft elongation and undulation of tone. He had left his arm spread across the table in the girl's direction as a sign for her to remain relaxed and to listen carefully to the itinerary.

'The theatre is the *Theatre De Chablau*. You will likely not have heard of it, but it is a nice theatre just off the Boulevard De La Villette, not far from here.'

The woman suddenly appeared by the table and dumped cups, a pot and spoons and a glass of coke on it. Jack acknowledged her as she turned and disappeared through the curtain to the back.

'You like coke,' he said, pushing the glass in the girl's direction. She nodded appreciatively and drew the glass nearer to her. Coffee was poured and Frederick casually raised the cup to his lips whilst turning to the reverse side of the menu. Jack raised a cup to his lips and his face dropped slightly.

'So…I can outline for you what will happen – the rehearsal…..' He hesitated a moment, striving for the word….'schedule. I think that is the right word.' The girl nodded confirmation. 'We will go from here soon to the rehearsal room. You will understand that it is not the theatre. It is too expensive to be rehearsing in the actual theatre. When we get to the room I will explain the movements and the…..' He paused again for the word drifting loosely in his vocabulary… 'Orchestrating… from the orchestra…You understand.' The girl nodded again and flicked her hair around the base of her neck. Frederick's eye rose momentarily from its menu. 'Good….so. The rehearsals are all arranged. The other dancers have received their ..itinerary…I think that is right.' He smiled and after a few quick exchanges with Frederick, finished his coffee, urging Frederick to his feet and to collect the girl's case in the process. As they left the café, Jack placed some silver coins in a saucer by the till.

They made their way down the street to a right turn, past a boulangerie where a woman in a black shawl was busily washing the paving in front of the door. Jack offered a word which she returned in a small exclamation and smile. They quickened their pace, rounding a corner to an incline where a black car stood parked just beyond some garage doors. Without hesitating, they crossed and the door was opened for the girl to take a back seat. Frederick occupied the passenger seat and Jack turned the key and steered the vehicle away from the kerb. He looked into the rear-view mirror.

'You are okay,' he confirmed, catching her eye with a vaguely quizzical expression. She nodded as they pulled away from the kerb. Recalling the route they had taken would have been impossible with so many turns down what seemed to be predominantly quieter roads and streets.

It was about ten minutes later that they came to a halt in an empty cobbled street flanked by a five-storey building and a derelict space full of refuse and broken glass. The men were out of the car in an instant and the door was opened for the girl to join them. She stood a moment, breathing the sharp Parisian air and scanning the dismal surroundings before following the men round a corner and along a quiet pavement for about twenty yards. They led her to a small alley which smelt of refuse and what could have been stale cider and finally stopped in front of a black padlocked door which Jack opened with his key.

Following Jack, they entered a narrow corridor which led to a door on the left. There was little to illuminate their path and the girl trod tentatively and brushed her hands gently against the wall surface as a guide. Finally, Jack found the light switch and with an expression of satisfaction brought a thin light from a light bulb hanging from a flex in the ceiling. A line of four clip-frame photographs were pinned to the wall. Each had young dancers posed in various stages of a routine and at the end, a picture of a masked face peering out from behind drawn theatrical curtains.

The door was opened revealing a huge room of almost mini-theatrical dimensions. A number of tables had been spread in a kind of random arc in the area in front of a 'mini' stage – a series of wooden blocks, painted in a rough and ready matt black, hastily drawn together for immediate effect. From a top corner a tiny beam of light made some headway through the gloom but died a death before getting anywhere near the 'performing' level. At the rear of the room, opposite the stage, was a banking screen of plywood with a number of small rectangles cut, apparently at random, into the wood. Jack indicated a seat just in front of the 'stage' with an invitation for them all to 'take the weight off their feet'. Frederick had been ushered to the side where a switch fed the room at least some illumination from two light bulbs hanging from the ceiling. Jack began.

'It isn't wonderful..but it is cheap. And for the rehearsals we have to save money. You understand?' The girl said nothing but nodded.

It wasn't wonderful – far from it. Thick black sheets had been nailed to a wooden beam behind the stage and a loose assembly of scarred tables and rickety chairs completed the scene. It was like a clear-out of some old village hall and far from the setting she had conjured up and romanticised in her mind; but she knew – and had been repeatedly warned by her tutors – that the theatrical world would often prove to be a harsh and demanding one; a world removed from the glamour of the great stages of Broadway and London's West End.

Having taken their places round a wobbling table, Jack proceeded to outline the 'production' details, giving at first a quick resume of the underlying idea and story-line based loosely on an old Spanish folk tale.

'It is the aftermath – of Civil War; a young girl is taken from her...comfortable environment by an unsympathetic and selfish mother to a strange world where she...'

He stopped, head-bowed to recall the word.. 'encounters the wicked Capitan Vidal.' His eyes widened – a mildly sardonic reaction to the story-line. 'The girl is miserable and alone..and can escape only in the fantasy world of her 'fairy tale'..what is the word?... 'obsessions'. She finds peace and then encounters a strange...I have checked out this word before... 'faun'..that is a ..mythology creature – half man, half goat..and she falls in love with the strange creature who eventually helps her to escape before he dies by the hunters of the Capitan. You understand the general idea and the feelings the dance is representing. Don't worry about all the details. We come to them later.' He pointed out that one of Frederick's roles was of musical-director and he would be correlating the orchestra's scores to the dramatic mood-swings that ...he hesitated again... 'brought the ultimate artistic quality in the performance.'

'It is a beautiful work,' he confirmed. 'You will find it a challenge, but with such lovely ideas I know you are the one to.....how do you say? 'carry it off". He smiled and proceeded to demonstrate – partly by gestures and partly in words – the pirouettes and movements that would bring soul to the piece and full expression in the ideas it conveyed. He explained that the other dancers had been issued with their schedules and were at that very moment working under the guidance of one of Paris's top teachers to be brought to the theatre for final rehearsals in some three or four weeks time.

The girl listened attentively and sank back on her seat for a minute. It had been a lot to take in in so short a period and Jack sensed that she had already been presented with more than she could likely cope with. He extended an arm and rested it lightly on hers.

'It's okay,' he said. 'You will feel more relaxed when we can start the rehearsals. And I would like now perhaps that we can try a few ideas...yes?'

The girl looked round the cold empty cell, the broken black beams of the roof a stern reminder, if any were needed, that her chosen path was never going to be an easy one.

'Good.'

Laying his hand along the base of her arm, he led her to a small alcoved area at the side of the room. A black screen had been hastily erected next to the dark hoardings in the corner. Jack reached down and withdrew a cellophane packet from a cardboard box, from which he withdrew a thin nylon dancing leotard suit and displayed it before her.

'This is one of the suits,' he said, brushing it down and handing it to her. 'It is of course fairly thin and brief, but remember that the essence of the work is the....fragility...of the young girl – she is.........' He hesitated, again unable at first to tap into the words he was searching for.. 'essentially lost in the evocative world of her imagination.' The girl took the suit and held it up for examination.

'So you can get changed there, behind this board. Then I'll just explain a part of a scene and maybe we can run through a few ideas. Okay? Frederick is arranging some music. We have a CD for the rehearsals but it will be a small band...orchestra...in the performance, okay?'

The girl nodded. It was far from warm in this dark empty room and it seemed a strange setting and strange circumstances for rehearsing a piece destined to be on stage in a theatre in a matter of weeks, but she reminded herself again that this was her chosen path: a world that owed as much to dusty cellars and make-shift props, as to grand stages with ornate canopies and elaborately decorated walls. She took the leotard and eased a screen in place to conceal her from view. A few moments later she emerged from the screen feeling cold and fragile in the skimpy nylon that clung to her young torso and bared legs.

'Good,' said Jack with a quick clap of hands and turn to Frederick somewhere up by the back screen. He moved the table and made space for the girl to approach the stage which was suddenly flooded in a brilliant cascade of silver light from two arced lamps, clamped to a metal trellis near the roof.

'That is better with the lights. Now we can see what we are doing.'

He turned to the stage and made a gesture with his arm.

'We perhaps take a scene from the first act. This is when your mother first tells you that you will be leaving the place that has been your home and you have that first feeling of confusion and at first a sadness.'

By use of hand signs and his curious English – fumbling and rudimentary at times, yet strangely eloquent at others – he indicated some of the technical features that would be appropriate in the scene and finally signalled for the music to begin. There was no sign of Frederick until, after a second or so's delay, he appeared toward the back of the room casually smoking a cigarette.

As he leant against the wall casting his gaze in the direction of the stage, the bars of a quite hauntingly beautiful piece of music suddenly swept into the room – filling every corner from roof to stage – a strain of artistic intent that had been impossible to envisage beforehand.

Jack had retired to the rear behind the screen to gauge the overall effect from a more appropriate vantage point, indicating one or two final suggestions before disappearing from sight, as the girl made her way onto the makeshift stage and with some trepidation began the arching, swaying movements that were hopefully going to be in line with the feeling Jack intended.

The approach was quite different from what she had been used to, where the demands of a piece had been more clearly dictated beforehand, but she could see that this, at least, would give her the chance to familiarise herself with the music and get an overall feeling for the mood. And as the seconds ticked into minutes and her self-consciousness gradually rescinded, the richness of the music's ebbs and flows quickly took hold, prompting movements that were some source of surprise, even to her. But this, she knew, was the *artistic* side to expression: an ability to respond there and then: to *improvise* freely, as the cliché would have it.

With the occasional shout of encouragement and odd direction from Jack from behind the screen, she found herself strutting, leaning and generally posing her body in arcs and postures in perfect harmony with the tones that filled the makeshift auditorium. There was little evidence of either of the men's presence throughout; a tactic designed to award maximuman unencumberence and the opportunity to express herself more freely.

It was clearly working. Rarely had the girl warmed so quickly and naturally to whatever piece was demanded of her, striking a level of confidence that would hopefully hold her in good stead for the remaining rehearsals.

It was after some eight or nine minutes that she finally resumed her position at the side of the stage, to be joined by Jack, who had made his way to the front to join her. There was no sign of Frederick, just the remnants of cigarette smoke drifting hazily in the left corner where he had occupied his viewing position. Jack extended a hand and with eyes that almost seemed to be dancing themselves, offered a congratulatory pat on the arm. 'Lovely........It was very good. You have already...captured.... the ideas. I'm sure you will be successful in the rehearsals and on the stage.'

The girl smiled, gratified to have 'passed' the initial auditioning process, happy to have been successfully apprenticed to the role. 'We will leave it there for today,' said Jack. 'Tomorrow we will work through the scenes and…' Again he stalled, trying to articulate the appropriate expression 'and…familiarise you more with the music and the ideas.'

It was with renewed optimism, an optimism that would have been difficult to envisage back in the car, that the girl turned to the screen to get dressed and reappear minutes later. 'Where's Frederick?' she asked, as Jack led her down the hallway to the outer door.

'Frederick has gone….for now,' he said with a smile as he switched off the light and made for the heavier door to the street. 'He has, at this stage, only to prepare the music and help with the general planning. He has left to see to one of the musical scores for one of the other teachers not far from here in another studio.'

In the car Jack had little to add as they drove to the café where they had met. They quickly got out of the car and made their way inside the café where a few words were passed between the woman and Jack. There was a nod and even a smile from the woman. Jack turned to the girl and placed the case at her side.

'We have a comfortable hotel room for you just down the street. It is not luxury…you understand, but it is clean and you will, I'm sure, be okay there. If there is any problem, I have had a word with Madame Daupant'…He nodded reasuringly in the direction of the counter, 'and she will be around.' He slipped a baguette concealed in a paper bag in her hand, which he gently patted as indication that it was 'on the house' and there was no need to pay. And with that led her to the street and with her case in hand he ushered her down a narrow alleyway which emerged as a tiny cobbled street. They passed a bookshop, a church and a small procession of bars. Beyond the second bar was the canopied entrance to a small hotel opposite a tiny arcade with tinny music and a flurry of red and orange lights.

'Basic' was the word, or maybe 'functional' - as lower-end-of-the-market hotel rooms in Paris are apt to be. The room was small – almost cabin-size. A functional bed protruded from a dour flower-arrangement background to a functional wardrobe that wavered uneasily on a slight incline in the threadbare carpeted floor. A frail white sheet was neatly folded back over a grey blanket to reveal a single pillow. As a matter of routine, she had switched on the tiny tv set that, through lack of space, had been placed on a chest of drawers, but had received only a bluish frosty effect crossed periodically by a series of broken horizontal lines of snow. It mattered little anyway, as it would all be in French.

She stretched herself out on the bed and extended her tired feet, revolving them slightly to confirm that the muscles were still working. To her left, a small window displayed the slanting roof of a neighbouring building and to its right, the evening sky which was already dark enough to herald the arrival of nightly illumination from the street below.

Having escorted her to her room and dumped the case by the bathroom door, Jack had dutifully re-congratulated her on her afternoon's work and promptly made his departure with a reminder that she should be back at the café early the following morning.

As she stood before the slightly slanted mirror and brushed lazily at the locks of auburn hair that shimmered and fell against the nape of her neck, the effects of a long and tiring day began to take their toll and for an hour, maybe longer, she lay on the bed slipping from slumber to semi-slumber until the former eventually took control, taking her to a world of swaying limbs and haunting melodies.

The following morning she made her way down the slightly rickety staircase to a small room where a cup of warm coffee and two wafery-looking croissants had been placed on a table in front of a chair. There were no other signs of life.

Having 'breakfasted' she stepped from the hotel into the brisk early morning air and made her way to the alleyway which led her to the street with the café, which like yesterday, stood untouched and unvisited until the jangles of the door brought first, the woman shuffling through the curtain to the counter and seconds later, Jack – this time alone – in from the street, smiling, extending an arm.

They took a table as Jack shouted a few words across, prompting the woman to busy herself with cups and saucers. Still smiling, Jack leant into the table and unfolded two neatly printed A4 sheets, angling them so the she was able to peruse them with him. Leading with his finger, he guided her down the page through some key moments in the performance's thinly worked 'plot', referring to certain manoeuvres and positions that had been pencilled in at appropriate points. She listened, followed his finger. The woman arrived with cups and coffee. Jack added that toward the end of the day's rehearsals there was the possibility that one of the other dancers may be joining them to put a few ideas together and practise some of the coordinated movements. Frederick was at that particular venue at that moment, sorting out some lighting problem that had occurred towards the end of the previous day's rehearsals.

After the coffee Jack ushered the girl to her feet. The doorbell stirred to life once again as they made their way to the car parked about thirty yards away up a hill.

The room was exactly as they had left it; the same loose scattering of tables and chairs, a glint of light in the top corner just about breaking its way through the rafters and the huge empty blocks of the makeshift stage backed by a series of bedraggled curtains and hastily erected screens at the side.

Jack scuffled his way past a number of packing cases to lead her to the same table as yesterday, where he took a seat, inviting her to join him. He withdrew the two sheets and began a more detailed explanation of the scenario, showing how the ideas stemmed from various stages of the synopsis. Various hand movements served to illustrate the flows of the piece until, happy that at least part of the performance had been adequately explained, he relaxed and in a more leisurely tone sought confirmation that she was comfortable with the prospect and with the expectations that had been laid before her. With clarification of one or two technical points, she nodded and allowed herself to be led to the side where Jack took a polythene sleeve and withdrew a second leotard. It was a particularly skimpy piece – moreso even than yesterday's – and she felt a return of awkwardness about wearing something so flimsy and revealing. Jack, quick to spot her hesitation, pointed out that the costume was simply a…. 'manifestation of her vulnerability' …..'emphasising her smallness..and of course her 'beauty'. He certainly had a flair for finding vocabulary as and when required, almost as if he had deliberately versed himself in certain terms, as a means of communicating the ideas of the dance. The girl held up the garment and brushed it down and then took her place once again behind the screen to prepare herself.

On her return, Jack had already made his way to the rear of the room towards the back screen. He cast a quick glance in her direction and with a final instruction, disappeared from sight.

The girl made her way onto the boxes and waited for the music. First came the lights, hitting the stage in a pool of silver that caused her to flinch and dip her eyes. The glare was fearsome, moreso than yesterday, and in the opening moments seemed to serve exclusively in drawing attention to her nakedness. The full lengths of her legs were starkly exposed, including virtually the whole of her buttocks, and a fair proportion of her waist and back. Her breasts swelled to their small pinnacles, the nipples taut against the skin-tight nylon.

For some moments she stood, hovering uneasily, like a rabbit caught in the glare of headlights – her state of near-nakedness seeming quite incongruous with the Spartan surroundings. And suddenly she felt cold, and alone, despite the sun-like heat radiating from the glare of lights.

It was with some relief that the first strains of music spilled into the room; a chance to relax and warm and sway to the sounds. Like yesterday, the only evidence of Jack's presence was the occasional instruction from behind the screen, usually in one of the quieter moments when the music waned and his few words would be audible alongside a slight whirring noise that was probably the electrics for the lights or possibly the music.

All in all and for the second day running, the rehearsal was proving to be a resounding success and it was about ten minutes or so later, that Jack emerged applauding enthusiastically and beaming the hugest of smiles.

'Bravo,' he said, making his way down to the front and extending an arm. 'Very good. You will be outstanding in the role, that is sure.'

He reached the table and took a seat, smiling widely and gently clapping his approval as she took her place opposite. Though pleased with her work and with the impression she had made so far, the girl was a little fatigued from her exertions and was relieved to recline for a moment and lay back against the seat rest. It was still early in the day and there were doubtless a number of further routines awaiting exploration. Jack allowed her some moments' relaxation before he continued.

'There is another idea in the performance,' he said, a slight hesitancy creeping into his normally assured tone. He looked to catch the girl's eye.

'You can see that the idea of the piece is the girl's release from the 'evil'..the spell that the Capitan holds over those he regards as his children.' He stopped, looking for confirmation. She looked and nodded.

'Well, one of the scenes is the final expression of the girl's freedom from him – it is in her imagination..in her 'fairy tale' world….you understand. And as an expression of her sense of release – there is a scene where the girl dances with the top completely open.'

He made a gesture with his hands toward an imaginary zip in his shirt and nodded at the girl's chest. She looked down finding the thin zip hidden by a thin sheaf of black nylon. She

had barely noticed it before and had assumed it was simply an
aid to putting the leotard on or taking it off.

'I know that you may be a little uneasy about your breasts
being exposed. I can understand. But let me say....it is only
for the one scene towards the end of the piece and in the end
you won't be alone, there will be other dancers on the stage
with you.'

The girl had little to say and could only hang her head,
rather like a child who has inadvertently spilt something down
her top. Jack leant forward, extending a reassuring arm.

'It just helps to convey the ideas – the expression of the girl's
desire for freedom.' His eyes rested heavily on hers. 'You
understand?' She nodded but he sensed that she might yet
need some convincing. After all – in dance-terms, she was still
relatively young.

His hand remained, placed firmly on her arm.

'If you are really unhappy and don't want to do it, you don't have
to. No-one is going to insist. It is essential that you are comfortable
with the piece in yourself or it will not work. So...just think about
it please...But remember – it *is* relevant to the story.'

He tried a different tack.

'Try to think of it as 'no big deal'.' He forced a grin at his
colloquial English. 'This is France remember.'

He held the grin in light of any reservations she may still be
harbouring. Maybe it was that that went some way to
convincing her – or that it was, after all, part of the story – or
maybe it was that *she* was being allowed to make the decision:
something that happened rarely in her theatrical world. She
looked at Jack and nodded.

'Okay,' she said. Jack gently tapped the back of her hand.

'Good. Thankyou,' he said. 'And please don't worry.'

He glanced down at his watch.

'I'm thinking it might perhaps be a good idea to practise that
routine now. You see what I am saying. Once you've done it
you will feel more comfortable with it and perhaps it will be not
so much on your mind in the future.'

There was little point in denying it.

'And remember,' he added finally, the tone of confidence fully restored in his voice. 'I'll be out of the way at the back behind the screen. It will be as if you are alone.'

He smiled and she managed to smile back.

'And I think that when we have run through this one practice scene, then we finish for today and you can have some time free. The other dancer won't be coming today, Frederick phoned earlier. They are still having some problems with two of the lights so have got a bit behind with the schedule. And anyway, you will have earned a break I think!'

She listened as he outlined the scenario and the dance movements that were required. He then led her once more to the stage and having loosely indicated how to adjust the sides of the leotard once the zip was lowered, he left her to prepare herself behind the screen and took himself off to the back of the room.

It took her a little time to arrange the costume correctly. It was a most unusual design and she'd never come across anything like it before. As Jack had indicated, the zip was first lowered to its entirety – unzipping her from just above the waist. The garment almost automatically eased apart, exposing her whole front, whilst staying tight to her skin by virtue of a slight gathering in the material near the shoulders. She looked sheepishly at her naked front – the trim curve in her waist leading up to the small mounds of her breasts, the nipples sharp and clear in the exposed air. The nylon could be adjusted slightly along the sides to ensure maximum exposure, whilst keeping the material tight above her hips and sides. That done, she turned and feeling rather like a young creature taking its first tentative steps into the wild, made her way into the room. There was no sign of Jack. He'd already taken his place behind the screen.

She stepped into the light, to all intents and purposes naked, except for the few remaining strands and stretches of nylon. She waited for the music, wanting the waves of sound to disappear in a series of arches and pirouettes – any reservations quickly vanishing. Only when the music waned and eventually died, did she draw herself to a closing bow with arms extended. This time there had been no passing instructions from the back, no sign of Jack, except for the spontaneous burst of applause as he reappeared from behind the screen and shouted his 'bravo'!

Minutes later and the girl was fully dressed and seated opposite Jack who had welcomed her reappearance from behind the screen with a gleeful extension of his hand. She took her seat and he complimented her once again on the level of artistry that was certain would make the performance a success. And he hoped she hadn't been too embarrassed.

She could afford a smile and waited to hear the plan for further arrangements and choreography. She was secretly pleased that she had agreed to do the scene; it had brought a new edge of confidence and shown her that the reservations many have for what is, after all, just another angle to artistic expression, are quite ill-founded. She even found herself prepared to ask questions and probe for details that twenty four hours ago she wouldn't have dreamt of raising. Jack answered her questions, but with exaggerated patience. She was, after all, still young and it wasn't a good idea to faze young dancers with too much to 'take on board' at these preliminary stages.

He confirmed that the following day they'd be working on two further scenes, probably nearer the beginning of the piece. The overall schedule was for a few more days rehearsal and then she would return home for a few days break, to return next week for the 'second phase' of rehearsals which would be with the remainder of the dancers, and would, after a few initial rehearsals, be transferred to the theatre itself.

They made their way down the hallway to the door and once out in the street Jack locked the door behind him and led her to the car. Once back at the café, he hovered a while at the counter and muttered a few words to the woman, who listened attentively and then disappeared behind the curtains. He turned and in customary fashion urged the girl to their table in the corner.

'Okay.' He paused a second and glanced at his watch. 'It is still fairly early and there are one or two things that would be useful to sort out a little later. I would like it if perhaps you could come here at....say two-o-clock. I need to see Frederick and get some details of one of the rehearsals, but I will be back. There will be no more rehearsing today, but I would like to discuss a few ideas from an earlier scene, okay?'

It meant she would have a few hours to herself, which after her earlier exertions, she would in fact quite welcome.

'Good.' Jack rose and with a light touch on her arm, thanked her again for her work and disappeared through the jangling door. The woman was nowhere to be seen.

Once back in the hotel she sat on the bed and dozed, trying to imagine the scene on the stage with an audience of..how many?..two, three hundred clapping and cheering. She smiled at the images of applause, the waves of haunting music and arched limbs.

She woke to find she still had time on her hands before she needed to meet Jack at the café.

The pavements were heavy with stall holders and the aromas of pancakes and garlic that seemed to mingle in the sweet sugary air. She had an eye on her watch, but with time on her hands and a few notes and coins of yesterday's advance from Jack firmly in her purse, she decided to reward herself a place at one of the neat little tables she had spotted in the cafes that seemed to run more or less the length of the lower end of the street. She took pride in taking time over her choice, letting it be known she was looking for a quieter establishment: one where the waiter might be prepared to show patience at her lack of French and be a little less brusque than some of his colleagues in the busier cafes appeared to be.

He in fact proved to be quite a charmer. Pretty girls – even the English variety – were more than welcome in this establishment. She perused the menu until she came across the 'pasta' section with the familiar 'bolognaise' clearly featured in the list. The waiter – resplendent in neat white shirt and black waistcoat – was convinced that her choice was indeed an excellent one and made it clear he was ready and waiting to oblige should she have any further requests. The food too was warm and welcoming and it was with something of the feeling of 'the sophisticated young woman in Paris', that she left what she hoped was an appropriate tip sitting on the plate and rose to make her way out into the street to head back towards the café for her meeting with Jack.

It was pretty much on the stroke of two-o-clock that she left the alleyway into the street and turned right to the café which even at this hour, stood as quiet and uninviting as ever. As the door jangled she hovered by the counter, waiting for Jack to make his appearance. There was no sign of the woman. There was no sign of anyone. She stood a little longer at the counter before deciding she may as well take a seat at the usual table. As she sat patiently, her arms folded neatly on the peeling yellow surface, she looked around the empty interior and glanced with increasing regularity at her watch; the minutes passed with still no sign of Jack. He must have got delayed at one of the rehearsals – not surprising when you considered the implications of directing a full-scale performance of dance set to orchestral music.

A moment later there was a stirring behind the counter as the woman appeared through the curtain. She stood a moment and looked across at the girl and then quickly disappeared again to reappear almost as quickly beckoning the girl over to her.

The girl rose from her seat and as she approached the counter, the woman held out a large brown envelope. She caught some of the woman's *'Les deux homes...mon't demande... de vous donner cela'* though of course it meant nothing to her. It was clear however that the envelope was for her and as she took it, the woman promptly disappeared through the curtain to the back.

It was an ordinary foolscap brown envelope and had her name written in neatly printed capital letters on the front. She turned it a few times in her hand and tore open the flap. Inside was a piece of note paper and a wad of bank notes. The girl looked around briefly to confirm that she was alone and then opened the note and read. It said quite simply:

*Helen.*
*Thankyou very much.*
*You are very artistic*
*and very sexy.*

*Jack (and Frederick)*

And that was all. She read the words again and turned the paper. The back was blank. She replaced the paper in the envelope and then withdrew the bank notes and leafed through them. They were of a high denomination – a very high denomination! For one her age she was suddenly unexpectedly rich. For some moments she just stood staring at the money, flicking the ends of the notes repeatedly through her fingers and then she pushed them back into the envelope which she replaced firmly inside her handbag.

She stood a while longer, making a point of waiting at the counter, just to confirm that there would be no sudden reappearance of Jack, or of anyone. As she waited, the more puzzling it all seemed to be. There was no sign of the woman. She hesitated, convincing herself that she was doing the right thing in abandoning the scene, bringing the bell its final jangling.

She stood on the deserted pavement, trying to consider what best to do, her hand clasping her handbag and squeezing it tightly. And then, casting a final glance along the cobbles to where the lane twisted out of sight, she made her way to the alley to return to the hotel and collect her case. It was all very strange.

It was some fifteen minutes later that she made her way along the cobbled street, passing the chemists shop and stopping briefly at the end of the turning towards *Rue De Lacarge,* where she scanned her eyes down the street one last time. All was quiet, almost as if the events of the last forty-eight hours had never existed. She reached the long series of steps and began their ascent, taking care not to slip or trip on the rugged stone.

Once at the top of the hill she turned her eyes to the small grassy lawns lined by tiny pathways and a series of fir trees. A number of benches were strategically arranged along the pathway to award views down across the city. All the benches were empty. She stepped across the lawn to the second one, where she took a seat and reached for her handbag. Confirming there was no-one in the vicinity, she slowly withdrew the envelope and opened the flap. Again, she brushed her fingers, once, twice, even three times across the notes – so many of them – and then quickly pushed them back in the envelope and replaced the envelope in her bag.

To her right, the rooftops and gables stretched into the well of the city. With something of a spring in her step, she took the other route, following the path that led to the *Metro* to take her back to *Gare Du Nord.*

# A Hole In A Wall

Dietmar Hessen leant back in the chair and tapped its neighbour for his nephew Johannes to take his place. Once settled, he reached to his right and took two thumb-nail glasses from a wooden chest, handing one to his nephew. Even such a simple act as this was proving something of a painstaking business these days; the years having slowed the simplest movements to prolonged, robotic manoeuvres and his nephew was obliged to wait patiently for the glass to be placed in his hand and the bottle of schnapps to be tipped lightly into it. That done, Dietmar relaxed a little, sighed and took a good long look at this strapping young nephew of his – he hadn't seen him for some months. He certainly had a lean, athletic look about him. A slightly hawkish nose and thin, piercing mouth gave him a somewhat dour expression - likely of no disservice to an ex 'National People's Army' - 'Peoples Police' Border Guard Officer of the GDR such as he was. He raised the glass to his mouth and then rested it neatly on the arm of the chair.

'So...you're keeping well uncle,' said Johannes, more a statement than question, casting a polite look to his right as he spoke.

'Oh....as you do...as you do...,' Dietmar replied, in customary aplomb. Which was in truth, about as good as got for him, in this, his seventy third year. His 'good days' – whatever and whenever they'd been – were some way behind him, leaving him, as with many his age, the heavily pockmarked scars of wartime and a stooping frame with little to contend with beyond an occasional venture into his garden and to the shop on the corner of their block.

He looked to his left and feeling a sudden surge of duty toward his young relative, reached once more for the chest and a dark beer in a small brown glass bottle.

'Have a beer Johann – I got them special; a good 'alt' beer.'

He handed the bottle to his nephew, who, not wishing to appear churlish, accepted it alongside the schnapps and began to pour the contents into the glass.

That done, the pair eased themselves once more into the warmth of the afternoon and the tiny square of garden that went at least some way to breaking the mould of High Rises and prefabricated slabs that were the hallmark of the surrounding area.

A short distance beyond the garden, the thick slabs of the Wall cut across their vision like a razor through a blood vessel.

'Admiring your handiwork?' commented Dietmar, nodding towards the bold interruption to their view.

'You credit me with too much uncle,' said his nephew, opting for politeness, his attention more focused on maintaining a slight head on the beer in his glass.

'Oh come come Johann, no need to be too coy now. We know you were one of the guiding-hands supervising the builders back in the early days. It's a fine structure, nothing to be ashamed of,' said Dietmar, with a wry smile.

'It seems to be doing its job,' said Johannes, contenting himself for the moment with the diplomatic line that would hopefully keep proceedings on a reasonably amicable level.

'Mm....so I'm told,' said Dietmar, raising his glass in exaggerated celebration of the fact.

Johannes returned the smile, but offered no rejoinder, accustomed, as he was, to a more sceptical appraisal of his and his colleagues' duties from people of his uncle's generation. Their lives, he knew, had been pretty much left in tatters by the war years – particularly in Berlin's latter days; and the subsequent march to 'liberation from the forces of evil' had done little to rejuvenate their spirits. And that aside, it was a pleasant enough afternoon and whilst off-duty his preference was to devote his attentions to relaxing without undue distraction.

He was equally aware, however, that his uncle had hardly invited him over to his garden for help in shifting a significant proportion of his schnapps and beer and to engage in a little light banter on the pros and cons of the Wall. But for the moment he would wait. You went with the tide on these occasions. You exerted the patience that a few months in the military were quick to instil. He took another drink and settled back in his chair.

It was some moments later that Dietmar leant a little closer to his nephew.

'Talking about the Wall. I heard a few more made it over in Wedding last week and another in Prenzlauer Berg. Is that right?' He spoke in the hushed tone one might adopt in discussing a neighbour's matrimonial difficulties. Johannes was silent for a moment, less from a sense of propriety than a lack of sound knowledge of the facts.

'I believe so,' he said, attempting at least some show of diplomacy.

Like many, Dietmar's head had been buzzing with tales and rumours and he was interested to get a more official 'low-down' while he had the opportunity.

'How hard is it Johann? I mean you hear tales of people being shot and mauled by dogs. Is that what really happens?' The voice was deliberately low-key, calculated to convey little beyond passing curiosity.

There was further hesitation from his nephew, again, as much a lack of surety of the facts as to any problem with his uncle's line of questions. This was, after all, his uncle's garden on a light sunny day with the pair of them enjoying a drink or two. What more could arise from a seventy year old man in discussion with his nephew?

'Some make it, that's for sure – but there's a lot more that don't, whatever you hear.' The words were flat, yet the warning was there. 'And of course, there are the implications for those left behind.' He twirled the glass in his fingers and brought it to rest on the arm of the chair.

'Don't tell me you're thinking of making a break for it uncle,' he said, with a grin.

Dietmar laughed, dismissing the suggestion with a swift drink from his glass – reminder enough of his generation's obligations to accept their lots in life with minimum fuss or complaint.

He reached for the schnapps bottle to refill his nephew's glass, filling his own in the process and replacing the bottle on the wooden chest. Their eyes returned irrevocably to the Wall. 'No, not a bit of it Johann. It's just that when you look and see so much bound in rumour and secrecy, it just makes you wonder what really goes on.'

He broke off for a moment, his attention seeming to focus on some point over and above the Wall: some building or interruption that appeared to have caught his attention.

Johannes was silent too; he had been quick to notice the drift in his uncle's eye and was disinclined to interrupt his thoughts.

It was some time before he returned to the more familiar territory of his garden and his observations on the tiny buds, the state of play of the border shrubbery and a dilapidated fence running halfway down the lawn until, wearying from such matters, Dietmar edged himself once more in his nephew's direction. What followed was most definitely for his ears only. 'Anyway Johann'. He shifted self-consciously in his seat as if to secure an appropriate position from which to continue, laying the glass to one side. 'There has been an interesting little development.'

Johannes turned to his uncle. So there was something after all. Dietmar returned his gaze to its chosen spot on the horizon. Then he made his announcement.

'Your cousins Klaus and Karl, his wife Annabella and Wilhelm are about to attempt an escape to the West.'

The words were delivered with a flatness that might have informed him of their intentions to join some local sports' club. There was a moment for the gravity of the disclosure to take its toll.

Johannes stared into his beer – lost in a sudden whirlpool of thought. He turned to his uncle.

'How..When?'

Dietmar shrugged but offered no immediate reply, allowing himself a little respite before he went on to explain how his grandson, Wilhelm, had discovered a hole in the bottom corner of the Wall whilst playing with his ball in the garden; how its appearance had been a matter of some conjecture; maybe from stress from some inner support or some tree rooting forcing a fracture – or just carelessness in construction, who knows?

'As far as Karl and Klaus are concerned, the only thing that matters is they see their 'ticket to freedom' handed to them on a plate,' Dietmar explained, his tone flat yet hinting at some greater intent.

He stopped and reached for the beer, draining it and ushering Johannes to 'do the honours' and bring two more from the bucket on the chest. Johannes dutifully obliged. He poured the contents under a smooth white topping and placed the glass to the side. Dietmar took a drink and again held his eye for some moments beyond the Wall.

'And that....as they say...is about it!'

He stirred the glass, eyeing its contents. 'Since then there has been little else thought about or talked about; just time spent making arrangements, trying to make contact with the 'underground bloc' for surveillance details and some intermediaries with contacts in the 'People's Resistance Movement'.'

He smiled at the routine simplicity of it all. 'There are changes almost daily – meetings and then more meetings, sometimes with some friend of Karl in Wedding. It seems with every new day comes a new idea. And then every night, the minute darkness falls – down to the Wall.'

He gave the glass a few twirls before continuing. 'They take it in turns to crawl through and do what little reconnoitring they can. But there's little to see in the dark, apparently just a stretch of what appears to be blocks or maybe ditches and then fencing close to the building opposite. Apparently, there's a light somewhere further down past a line of posts close to the Wall – a search-light – so they wait and count it before it appears again in the same direction. And then the next night the same again.'

He raised his glass, the cool liquid soothing the dry edginess in his throat. Johannes had remained silent. For a moment, he seemed reluctant to pick up the story.

'I realise you may be surprised that I'm telling you all this, but these things are never as straightforward as they seem, particularly in such dangerous circles as they are moving.' He hesitated, tapping the glass thoughtfully against the arm of the chair, his head bowed in its direction.

'The trouble is Johann.....my children are somewhat younger in heart than in years.'

His face relented to a half-smile. He nodded towards the foot of the garden, inviting Johannes to follow his gaze.

'The fact remains that the monstrosity we see there each and every day of our lives, dividing us – separating us like lepers, doesn't just cut across our vision...it cuts across our minds too. Forcing us to see only what we want to see.'

He broke off a moment, waving the tilted glass to catch the sun's refractions in a series of glints and sparkles.

Johannes had always wondered why his uncle always chose to ignore the suffix of his name; maybe a private joke or a simple labour-saving device beloved in older people or maybe he just didn't realise.

'And then later, each night they huddle together under the kitchen light – Wilhelm too. And talk in excited whispers....clinking glasses to nights in the Ku'damm or Kempinskis, bockwurst and Coca-Cola at imbiss stands, evening strolls in Tiergarten, Dance-nights for the new music – the 'beat' music of America.'

He grinned his own imaginary rhythms of the New Music of the New World, the grin broadening to a gentle laugh. 'My children have the edge on me there, I have to say. My eyes are fading along with my ears. I cannot see so clearly into such distances as they can.'

He leant back, taking a welcome breath of warm afternoon air. 'But I suppose it is that they are young, whereas I am old. And at the end of the day, that is the difference between us.' He turned to Johannes and smiled.

'They want me to go with them.' The idea was evidently a source of some amusement. 'Kept begging me at first, still do. 'Come papa..you must come...things will be so much better over there, you know.' They like to tell me about these contacts they have, some ex-friend of Klaus - finance friend, works for a building firm in Charlottenburg and Annabella's sister – a waitress somewhere – some restaurant on the Kurfurstendamm I think she said. Every day the same – 'You must come too. We don't want to leave you here. It will be easy, you'll see."

He chuckled; the smile cutting into the bones of his face and drifting to his lap.

Johannes was silent, his uncle's words leaving little opportunity for any appropriate reply.

Dietmar turned again to his nephew and tapped him gently on his elbow.

'So....Johann. I'm thinking that a little help may be of some service here.'

He stopped and looked deep into his nephew's eye.

Johannes's thoughts were suddenly racing. The fact was that for all their trials and tribulations, all the horrors they'd witnessed, people like his uncle had little concept of the reality of these things. That the kinds of favours he was imagining were impossible – particularly in current times – not to mention the implications for the family members.

For the first time he gathered himself to speak, turning grim-faced to his left.

'Uncle ____'

He was stopped by a light pat of the hand.

'Johann...Johann...please.'

The hand remained, resting nonchalantly on his arm. Johannes found himself once more reduced to the roll of passive listener.

'Relax.'

Dietmar had repositioned himself in the seat of the chair. The words that followed were as if from a second voice somewhere deep inside his head.

'There are times Johann when perhaps our eyes have the edge on our children's in these matters.' He nodded in the direction of the lower garden.

'You see the Wall?'

Johannes nodded.

'I think you have found a breach in it....Am I right?'

There was a pause, during which Johannes stared blankly at the concrete slabs that severed their vision; the words had somehow disappeared.

'Come come Johann – no need to be coy now. I think we both realise that such a fine structure needs regular and thorough surveillance or how can we be sure that it will be able to do its job eh?' He stopped and turned to take a good hard look at his nephew who thought for a moment and stuttered, 'Of course uncle.'

'Of course,' repeated Dietmar. 'And having discovered a little problem, I would imagine you're duty-bound to report it immediately. For failing to do so could lead to a number of much greater problems for you.'

Johannes was silent.

'I think so,' said Dietmar, taking advantage of his nephew's hesitation to do his answering for him. 'Don't worry, I seated us deliberately here out of view of the neighbours. No-one will get to know about your little visit.'

Dietmar drank the remainder of his beer and had barely removed the glass from his lips before he reached over to the wooden chest.

'Now, another beer Johann, and a schnapps too I think.'

'Thankyou uncle,' said Johannes, staring hard in the direction of the Wall with an expression of some relief.

# Extract From A Schoolboy's Diary

I put on my striped tie, collar shirt and blazer. There's a white badge on the blazer pocket with something like a castle sewn in cotton and some words written in Latin sewn underneath. Sometimes in assembly the headmaster says the Latin words aloud and talks about them. I don't often look at the words myself.

This morning I had my cup of tea, slice of toast, then lifted my bag onto my shoulder and after checking the coins in my pocket and my key, I made my way as usual along the avenues. I shivered and my face felt sharp and tender in the cold February air. A few cars passed and a bus crammed with teenagers in uniforms. I gave them a quick glance. I wouldn't like to have to catch the bus. The air was misty, making the houses in the distance seem ghost-like; until when I got near to them they cleared to the usual patterns of brick and glass without signs of movement or life. Heidi Swarbrick lives in one of these houses but I don't know which one. I've never seen her going in or coming out of any of them.

When I got to school I went round the back by the small garage-like shed in a quiet corner next to the back field. The side of the shed faces a line of small green bushes and trees. It's very quiet there behind the shed. I reached down the bottom of the wall for my little green tennis ball that's tatty by now, with wide grey patches scarred into the stringy surface. I kicked it repeatedly against the side of the shed. The idea is not to let it rebound passed me. I have to shuffle around and move quite quickly to stop this happening. I sometimes pretend I'm a footballer playing for some team. This morning I managed fourteen before the ball passed me, which was pretty good. When it was time I put the ball back in its little secret hole at the bottom of the shed wall where no-one will find it and then I went into the building.

In registration I sit four desks down the third row from the left. When everyone who's there has said 'yes miss' there's a short silence whilst she writes the numbers in a little box. Sometimes, like this morning, I get to take the register back to the office. I stopped for a minute on the stairs and opened the book to look at the huge page of tiny squares. It seemed like there were a few thousand of them, with a few hundred small red diagonal lines from top to bottom with some black circles, all drawn neatly in the squares, creeping across the page, and days, weeks and months. All the classes are kept neatly together, in a line, in a box, on a shelf in the secretary's office.

In a long straight line we walk quietly down the stairs to the bottom and turn left to the hall, where we stand in silence in straight rows – a few hundred of us – brown, blond, black and some ginger heads all lined neatly from side to side, slowly filling the hall from corner to corner, front to back. We have to sing a hymn. I'm not religious and as it's nothing to do with learning subjects I don't see why we sing a hymn. I once asked a teacher why and she said it's because you have to. I don't sing and neither does nearly everybody else, so when we sing the hymn no-one's singing, and all you can hear is the piano and a few teachers who sing to set an example. Sometimes everything stops halfway through and the piano stops playing and we're told angrily that we aren't singing and then for a while some more will sing until time passes and they can slip back into not singing. Sometimes we're asked 'why' we aren't singing, though we're not allowed to answer the question. After the hymn we have to bow our heads to pray to God. I don't see why we have to do this either, and I don't, but it doesn't matter because no-one knows whether you're doing it or not, so they don't have to worry about that. When we look up again someone speaks to us about something they say is important, but I'm not usually listening.

After assembly the school sometimes seems a bit sleepy. This morning the air was bright and everything seemed to settle into the brightness drifting in from the cold morning outside. It made sharp white beams across the rooms and made the faces pale like ghosts. We had Science. We opened our books to a display of the split stem of a plant – its innards were clear and lines and labels explained how the plant lived. Outside, lines of trees and little bushes and hedges bordered the avenue down to the main road. They were alive; you could tell just by looking at them. But I don't usually notice them because I don't like plants. They don't do anything. I looked at the cut open plant in the picture. It didn't look much – cut open like that on the page. We had to draw it and label it. It took a while but that was okay, I can copy things down like that quite easily. As usual I looked at Heidi Swarbrick who sits on a left hand bench halfway down the room. In Science she's side-on to me with a line of hair hanging down her right cheek. I was thinking about her as I drew the plant's split and the clearly lined innards inside the sliced opening. As usual we had to answer the questions under the picture and whilst I was doing that I took a few more glances at Heidi and at the sliced open head and open brain on the poster above her.

In History there were people spiked on long pointed poles stuffed up their innards; their blood spouting in red fountains as they cried out before dying. It was in a cartoon book called 'Bringing History To Life'. We drew pictures of people with poles inside them and had to write about it. I didn't have any coloured pencils and no-one had one to lend me so I had to draw the blood in grey. Some of the class showed their pictures to each other, but I was busy finishing mine off so I didn't bother.

At break I went to my usual place by the wall at the side of the playground. I like it there but this morning it was cold; the wind cut like a razor, making me bury my hands deep in my coat pockets and my head in the collar. I don't kick my ball against the shed wall at break because some of the boys might want to come over and join in. I stay standing by the wall where I can watch the rest of the kids laughing in their little groups, munching their crisps and chucking their crunched up bags on the floor. One boy slipped and landed on his bum which made us all laugh. Shortly after, another boy came over and made my tie a bit tighter for me - a bit too tight - and I choked a bit at first. I couldn't loosen the knot and had to put my finger through the loop and pull it to make it a bit easier.

For Art we have Mr. Dyson, or Vince we call him because he looks like Vincent Price. He doesn't say much and likes elbows. They say he draws them a lot and likes to touch them and likes to touch sixth-form girls there and it's sexual. But I don't know any sixth-form girls, so I don't know. We had to draw something which gave a feeling like an emotion. I drew a tiny dog and a dustbin and a tree with no leaves at the other side of the paper. I did it in pencil and made the dustbin bigger and had things sticking out of the top. Some of the boys added bits for me, but I rubbed them out because I preferred it as it was and then I put my name on top.

On the way to English Simon Creace came up to me. He isn't really my friend but he sometimes speaks to me. I don't always hear what he says though because he tends to speak quickly and sometimes jumps up and down in front of me while he's speaking and I can't understand him. And then he runs off laughing. He's a bit weird, but they say his parents are drug addicts. The English teacher's Mr. Payne – Al Payne. He's tall and wears silver suits and has a long hanging face like a bloodhound. He walks quickly round the room and when we write something he says we're building the blocks of communication, so we can manipulate them and be part of a process. I don't understand what he means and we read quite a lot of poems which I don't understand either; but he says you don't have to understand them – you just experience them. He says it's like plugging your mind into an electric socket. We once read a book called 'Great Expectations' and I quite liked the first bit when it was quiet and a bit spooky in a graveyard. But then there was this boring woman in a house and an old fashioned girl and it got a bit boring and I couldn't understand it. At the end of today's lesson he gave me back some writing I'd handed in for homework. I'd written it quickly behind the skip because I'd forgotten about doing it. I didn't think about what I was writing and just put down the first thing that came in my head. He wrote *'Thankyou John I really enjoyed reading this'*. I don't know why he enjoyed reading it because it was crap.

Lunchtimes can sometimes drag. We have to eat our lunch in the packed lunch room. As usual I ate my sandwich from my plastic box first. I save my chocolate biscuit for when I sit on top of the skip later, otherwise some of the others come up to me for a bite or a few bites of it. It seems they aren't allowed to have them, so they like mine. But I only have the one, which isn't really enough to go round. So I save it to eat it later. I tell them they can have my apple if they want because I don't really like apples, but they don't seem to like them either. When we've finished our lunch we go in the playground. I like to run from the wall of the school to the skip not far away. They put the skip out of the way behind concrete walls near a few trees. This is where they throw the big rubbish – not paper and stuff like that, but bigger things and it never seems to be emptied, or I've never seen it being emptied. I like to think about what might be in there. So when I'm running from the school wall I take a run-up and reach up with my arms over the top and pull myself up to sit on top and look inside to see if there's anything half-decent; you never know when you see things like chairs and those projector-things sticking out. But I never find anything worth taking. I like to sit up on top though, half hidden behind the trees and look out across the tarmac. The top of the skip is my place; no-one comes near and from there I can see the other kids across the playground, pulling and teasing and fighting each other. Heidi Swarbrick hangs out with her mates in a little slot between the trees about forty yards beyond the skip. There are usually about five of them. They pout against the tree trunks and tell tales and laugh and repeatedly check themselves in mirrors, flicking their skirts around in the cold. Sitting on top of the skip I can see them for a while whilst I'm checking under old chairs to see if anything's hidden underneath. But I never find anything and in the end I just dump the chairs back. Today on the way back into school I got a bit too near two boys who were extending their arms like a plane and they caught me on the back of my head and then two others playing football without a ball, accidentally caught me on the shin; but there was no blood and it didn't hurt too much.

In French we're supposed to say things to each other, which I don't like doing. The others know I don't like doing it and tend to leave me alone. In one lesson a few months ago Heidi Swarbrick was made to sit at the desk next to me - which is always empty – because she kept talking to her friends. The other kids made cheering noises as if they were pleased and they giggled to each other as she took hold of her bag and moved slowly across the room towards me. She kept facing away at her mates – and perched herself on the far corner of the seat, deliberately slowly, still looking away from me, smirking at her friends. I just looked down at my text book - at the picture of a tall thin waiter with a wide moustache holding his tray out with a collection of words on it. The idea was that we should say things to each other in French, but she wouldn't and we didn't. She just looked glum and refused to say anything, keeping her head turned away the whole time. I didn't mind. I wouldn't have known what to say anyway. I don't like conversations much. That was some time ago.

Today after French we went back to our form rooms to get what's called an 'interim report', which is a little sheet of paper with four boxes for each subject. The boxes go from 'good' to 'bad' and the teachers put a tick in one of the boxes for each subject, depending on whether you were good, fairly good, bad, or fairly bad. Most teachers put ticks in the second box which means fairly good. Most of my ticks weren't so good, except English, but he'd got it wrong as usual. Under the line of boxes there was a space for the form-teacher to put a comment and she'd put *'John could do quite well but he must contribute more and push himself more.'* They always tell me I should contribute more. The trouble is I can't, but they don't seem to realise this. Some of the kids compared their number of 'good's and 'very good's. I just put mine in my pocket and put my things away in my bag. When we were sitting quietly in our lines and rows, we were allowed to go home. I took hold of my bag making sure I hadn't left anything and, as usual, made my way along the corridor to the library.

I went to one of the seats against the back wall and peered out of the window onto the grounds and the pathway down to the gate. The skies were getting dark now as the school emptied onto buses and off down the road. Little clusters of kids busied themselves with their tales of the day and girls strode arm in arm, their skirts high, waving at their friends, who waved back at them at the gate, ready with their stories and their plans for the evening. I always let my school mates leave first, leaving the school in silence for me and one or two home-workers and the librarian, who's usually busy with a small pile of books and their tickets. A long thin tube lights the library in brightness like an operating theatre, which after a while makes outside seem almost black.

Today I flicked through one of the photo books. I like the black and white ones best. Things look better in black and white. One book had photos of Paris taken at night. You could see the lights of cafes like little white stars dotted against the dark streets. And a market place, emptied of people was littered with crates, cardboard boxes and other rubbish chucked away across wet cobbles partly lit from the corner street lamp.

After about half an hour the librarian came over to me and stood watching me looking at the pictures. She didn't say anything at first and then she asked me if I liked the book. I said yes. She said she'd noticed me in the library each evening and it pleased her to see someone coming in to see the books after school. I didn't say anything and then she said I could take the book with me if I wanted. I told her I didn't have a ticket but she said it didn't matter; the book was quite an old one and no-one ever took it out anyway and if I wanted I could take the book and keep it. I looked down at the pages, at a picture of rubbish piled outside a grocer's shop in the rain and I ran my fingers across the cool surface of the paper, as smooth as marble. I thanked her and closed the book and clasped it under my left arm, which meant my bag could hang on my right shoulder.

Darkness had crept along the corridors and rooms as I made my way out into the empty drive. I had to clutch the book tightly under my arm to stop it slipping because it was a bit heavy. It was dark as I walked down the path and out through the gates and made my way back as usual along the avenue where the houses, once covered in mist and now almost in darkness, were still without signs of movement or life. I stopped for a minute in front of one of the houses and looked at its blank, empty windows. Maybe this was Heidi Swarbrick's house. Maybe she was in there now in the back kitchen, making something for tea. I briefly imagined myself in the house too, standing in the front lounge looking out onto the avenue. Then I turned away, and with my book clasped under my arm, I walked on.

# Into Africa

Meryl Whittaker and her husband Gerald stepped awkwardly through the narrow door of their cabin. They stepped awkwardly as the doorway on this particular cabin was somewhat narrower, or seemed to be, than on previous boats. Meryl re-iterated the point most times she stepped in or out of it. Gerald conceded the point but reminded her that they'd opted for a class lower accommodation this time, on account of this cruise being a touch more exotic, taking them to more far-flung parts than before. Meryl conceded that; but wherever you were in the world, you still had to get in and out of your door, and with this one she almost had to turn sideways and face the door frame to do it. And she was no spring chicken any more. She was in fact somewhere in her sixties and although slightly overweight in frame, still agile enough for most of the demands of their annual cruise.

'The Sun Kiss Of The Seas' wasn't expensive Gerald, but getting in and out of the cabin was easier than this.'

'Well, maybe – maybe not. Anyway, you've got out and later on you'll more than likely get back in again, so never mind.'

She took his arm, partly out of habit and partly for support, as they stepped their way along the maroon carpeted aisle past the line of brass-handled, cream coloured doors of the other cabins.

It was eight o clock. They liked to be out of their cabin by eight o clock, so they could make their way to the restaurant and be seated and breakfasting at about quarter past.

They were seasoned travellers, having cruised coastal Europe and the Med extensively over the last ten years or so. But the wider world beckoned and this time they'd plumbed for a more extravagant two week option from the brochure. It had involved a flight to Egypt first, which had caused them both a bit of concern. But they'd managed to get there safely and most of the people on the plane had been white anyway, rather than terrorists.

They reached the bottom of the stairs and stood in a short queue before the attendant – one of scores of smiling Philipinos – took them to their place in the restaurant. Once settled in their places with polished glass and china and freshly laid doilies, full breakfasts duly arrived for the pair to prod and poke at, as, North East Africa slipped its way contentedly through the port-hole on their left hand side.

The morning sun, having broken above the bush and dunes of the eastern plains, had found its way through the boat's narrow port-holes, bringing a stark 'Hopperesque' light-effect to the dining room – the 'Diners In The Morning' cast either in shade or in brilliantly formed pools of sharp sunlight. Unfortunately it was a bit too much for Meryl – shining right in her eyes like that; she was struggling to even see the fried bread, never mind being able to cut it and get it on her fork with a slice of sausage and some egg yolk. She was forced to lean back so she was out of its way and just hope that the egg didn't drop off her fork onto her clean slacks, that she'd bought specially. Gerald was sympathetic but at a loss as to what to do. The waiter, on a routine visit to the table, offered them another place sharing a table, but they were seated now and had already poured their tea. Unfortunately he could do little about the sun. Gerald pointed out that this was Africa, as the waiter busied himself sweeping away their crumbs. It had left Meryl a little weary and a quick lie down was required before the top deck could be tackled. Gerald took the opportunity to take a little morning air in a wander round the 'A deck' sun-beds and whirlpool.

He returned to the cabin to find his wife asleep on the bed, her arms folded gently across her midriff, looking, in the semi-diffused light, like a freshly-laid corpse. His wander had taken him past the Whirlpool and Sunken Bar to 'Exterior Walkway –

Right', where he'd bumped into Alice and Tom from the Piano Bar last night. They were claiming their place in the 'Covered Sundeck – Right' near the servery for convenience. Tom had a bout of sun-sickness and had given breakfast a miss. His wife was okay but very hot. It was already boiling out there. He strolled past the Rameses and Abu Simbel suites and then down the steps to the entrance to 'Forty Five to Ninety' - and air-conditioning, which was more than welcome on a day such as this.

Soon Meryl surfaced for her paracetemols; the sun had given her a bit of a head. Gerald settled into the chair for ten minutes with the newspaper. He wouldn't start the crossword just yet; it annoyed Meryl when he did that because she didn't get the chance to leap in with some of the easier ones. On the boat they usually saved it till later in any case, when they'd settled themselves in the sun-chairs. He checked his Stars. It said he could discover something that could be to his advantage. He read it out to Meryl and they discussed what it might be. He then read hers out as she applied the last few touches to her face. They donned themselves in lightweight slacks and tops and equipped themselves with hats, creams and lotions and camera. It was well into the morning as they eased themselves a little awkwardly through the cabin doorway where she took her husband's arm as they made for the door to the deck.

As usual, the heat struck like a hammer, instantly drawing her hands to her bonnet which nestled precariously on its base of candy-floss perms. Wincing from the light, they found their way along the sun-deck to 'Covered Sun-Deck, Left' - 'Sun-Deck Right' would be too full by now, they'd found that out by experience.

Easing themselves gently into their chairs and reclining so that their hats were correctly angled and their seats secure, they took a newspaper and magazine and gently fanned themselves against the appalling sun, watching a handful of seagulls or buzzards, or whatever they were, flying in small concentric circles, seemingly oblivious to everything.

Mind you, so far, and this was only an initial impression; apart from the sun, they quite liked Africa. There was some nice scenery and there was certainly a lot of space. And the people were very friendly; they often waved as they stood on the river bank watching the boat go sailing past them. It was a very historical place too. Some of the things they'd seen went right back into history, back as far as the Bible the courier in the blue uniform on the coach had told them. And you could tell that when you actually saw them in the flesh; then you realised. It was quite different from seeing them in a book, and there were certainly lots of things to see. It was just a pity about the sun.

The day before the boat, had been the 'Treasures Of The Desert' coach tour. That was a very good way of seeing things because the courier explained it all and the coach's polaroid windows made it darker, which meant the sun wasn't so bright.

They went past some very interesting sights. They'd stopped at one place where there were men with camels. Gerald said he wouldn't mind having a ride on one. Meryl told him not to be so daft. He made a joke about her bringing her mother with her. The men who were wrapped in sheets and had big smiles, offered them a ride – but you would have to pay. Gerald told Meryl she must have the camera ready when he was stuck up in the air between two humps of one of those camels. She wanted to know what he planned to do when it went out of control and went galloping off across the desert with him on top; what was he going to do then? He told her not to be so daft. Instead of riding camels they'd opted for a cup of tea, a chocolate cake and a sit down. Fortunately they had their fans with them and they were able to sit down in the shade.

They were struggling a bit with the day's crossword – but knew that once they'd got a few more, others would follow – it always worked that way. They'd been thinking about four across...'homely...beginning with d..' They finished off their tea and chocolate cake and screwed the silver wrapping papers into the ash-tray in time for the next part of the tour, which was a 'walk-tour' through a series of huge grey pillars where it was said the floor had once been covered with precious stones.

Gerald looked down and scuffed the dust on the floor with the edge of his shoe. The pillars towered above them like huge concrete pistons – their supporting corners broken and crumbling under the centuries of sun.

Gazing upwards made Meryl twist a shoe heel on the loose stones, but fortunately nothing broke. Gerald wanted to take a picture and was standing wrestling with the camera because the film didn't seem to be wound on. Meryl had used it last and was adamant that she'd wound it and it had clicked – so it wasn't her fault - don't go blaming her. She had a look at it and flicked the little lever. Something clicked. He stood aiming the camera as she stepped across the dusty ground and stood in front of one of the pillars. He told her to smile and she told him to hurry up, the sun was terrible standing there. The guide told them that evidence of hieroglyphics could still be seen in places in some of the pillars, though you had to look closely. They walked over to one or two of them to get close and leant forward to see what they could see – but nothing was very clear – they must have been worn away over all those years with the weather, or maybe it was the wrong pillar. The guide went on to tell them that down the river there were twenty two tombs that hadn't been discovered and rumour had it that a mosquito had flown out of the tomb of Tutankhamen. Neither Gerald nor Meryl liked mosquitoes.

They bumped into Bob and Cassandra (Cassie) who'd been wondering how they'd built the huge pillars. No-one could guess and then Meryl took a picture of them both in front of the coach. In the skies above, a handful of buzzards circled or flew wildly into the winds, only to return on the trough of the next, where they seemed to hover in apparent anticipation.

Meryl stared up at them for a second – but only for a second – the sun was too bright. She asked Gerald what they were. He told her he thought they were buzzards. You get them in the desert. They hang around, waiting for things that are dying.

It was another peaceful day in North Africa. Beneath the sun and a small circle of buzzards, the boat passed shimmering greens interspersed with thin lines of golden sand and the small huts and homes of the valley, as the cruisers laid back, wafting warm air across their faces with fans or newspapers, their eyes closed against the sun. Gerald scratched his nose; Meryl wiped her head. Soon after, they got up. You can only spend so much time in the sun. It can get too much.

She took Gerald's arm and he guided her along the rail of the boat to entrance 'One to Fifty Six'. As they passed a forest of palms and a small temple built in the desert rock formation, he warned her about slipping on some grease, or melted sweet or whatever it was that seemed to be smeared on the deck. He guided her through the door and down the steps to safety and relief.

Back in the cabin Meryl lay on the bed with her arms folded across her chest. Gerald sat in the chair and added two more to the crossword. They'd done over half of it by now, but this was when it started to get a bit tricky – there were always three or four that they just couldn't seem to get. Meryl wasn't going to wear her blue blouse at the 'Night Of The Pharaohs'. She'd got a stain on it earlier, probably a drop of gravy. She'd probably wear the white one with the flowers on it. Gerald said he might dress up as a Pharaoh – or even Cleopatra – you never know. Meryl told him not to be so daft. She was definitely going to take it easy on the Bacardi and cokes though, that was for sure, after all this sun.

She got off the bed and took some postcards off the shelf. They were only sending about five. They'd written three of them and she sat on the other chair and took her biro from her handbag to do the next. She wrote that Africa was quite a nice place – the food had been quite good, though a little rich on occasions and there was quite a lot of entertainment, but it was very hot. Over a hundred degrees they said, at some points of the day. She asked him if he wanted to add anything; he said 'no'. She finished the cards and put them back on the shelf for the post later.

They usually had lunch at the open deck café, as long as it wasn't too hot. It was well shaded and they ordered straight from the buffet which meant they could just have as little as they wanted. They met up with Alice and Tom in the queue. Tom was feeling a little better and felt up to a spot of lunch, but nothing too rich. Alice had certainly caught the sun. She looked like glazed gammon straight from the oven. They'd both done a 'China And The Far East' cruise last year. That had been quite an experience and the food – there'd been so much of it – almost too much at times.

They reached the hot-plates in the queue and checked the offers. Gerald plumbed for sausage and chips, Meryl had just a few pieces of braising steak in gravy with just a little mash. Tom had decided to stick to a sandwich – just in case. Alice hadn't been able to make up her mind and decided to follow Meryl's example. Fortunately the gravy wasn't too rich; they hadn't put too many onions in it this time. Eating makes you hotter of course, and they had to fan themselves continuously just to try and keep themselves a bit cool. They had wondered about taking lunch in the restaurant where it was air-conditioned but you can't always be sure what you want at lunch and it helps if you can see it, so you can decide how much you actually want on your plate. And as Tom had pointed out, it can be a bit chilly in the restaurant when you come in out of the sun and that can bring on a cold if you're not careful.

Gerald dropped a bit of sausage on the deck and joked that the buzzards would be down for it any second. Meryl told him to pick it up then quick and he asked her if she fancied a bit of buzzard for tea. She slapped his arm and told him not to be so daft. Tom went to get the cups of tea.

They took their time over the tea, relaxing back in the easy-chairs, occasionally casting their eyes over the rail at the passing river banks. Sand banks and small clusters of palms, occasionally broken by a small cluster of huts, provided most of the scenery. Tom pointed out that there was probably quite a lot of poverty round these parts and they agreed that this was quite likely. None of them fancied a pudding though Alice toyed with having an apple.

They returned for a while to 'Covered Sundeck Left', though there was some space at 'Covered Sundeck Right', but it would have been a bit of a squeeze which can make it uncomfortable and it would be very hot there too – particularly at this time of day. So they found seats at sundeck left and sunk down and closed their eyes for ten minutes to let their lunch go down.

Gerald added two more words to the crossword. Tom told them 'to cut' was.. 'lacerate'. They'd never have got that one. That meant eight down must be 'confuse' as they'd thought. Alice left them after only a few minutes. It was getting too hot - she was wary of heat exhaustion. Tom offered to return to the cabin with her but she said he didn't have to, she'd be okay.

Shortly after that, the boat came to a standstill. There was an announcement over the tannoy that due to some river congestion, which wasn't unusual at this time of year, there'd be some delay – possibly up to a few hours. It was to do with a problem with the lock, which could only accommodate one boat at a time. They wondered why they had locks, it was so flat. Tom said that where you get a lot of boats there were bound to be problems.

The congestion problem appeared to be a familiar one to the locals, who suddenly appeared alongside the boat from all directions, ready and equipped to take full advantage. Before they'd been stationary more than fifteen minutes or so, the riverside was hectic with traders eager to pursue a little commerce with their more-than-affluent Western guests. Lines of smiling males shouted offers of robes and shirts of various colours and sizes – all conveniently pre-wrapped in cruise-friendly polythene bags clutched at the ends of extended arms in exchange for five pounds. Five pounds was the going-rate of all produce available on the banks of the Nile; whether due to comparability of their wares, or limitations of their English, wasn't easy to establish.

Meryl, Gerald and Tom clung on to the rail and peered over the side to observe the scene below.

'Five pounds....Five pounds only......'

Even the circle of buzzards joined in the furore, intrigued at the prospect of international trade shaping up beneath them.

Gerald wanted to know what sizes they had – and shouted his enquiry down; the men grinned back in agreement. Arms flailed in the air as plastic bags flew at them and over their heads; one or two pitching a direct hit into the whirlpool behind. Meryl saw one top in pale blue that one of the men held open in outstretched arms; but she needed to check what it was made of because of her skin. She shouted down whether it was cotton or nylon. The man smiled and confirmed the price. Five pounds for a top, when you're not sure whether it'll bring you out in blotches, needed thinking about. She wasn't sure. Gerald had an idea that rather than give him money, what about the old mobile phone that they'd got in the room? They'd been given a new one for Christmas, but had left that one at home – they rarely used either of them in any case and weren't sure that the old one worked properly. But the men might like it; it still worked after a fashion and they could store some names and numbers on it. Or they might like just pressing the buttons and seeing the numbers light up on the little screen. He went to get it and returned a few minutes later. He leant up against the rail and held it high in the air, pointing at it.

'Mobile...mobile phone – You have...for blue top!'

There was a hint of understanding. The man smiled and raised his hand shouting something that none of them could understand. In a single fling of his other arm, the top was released into the air and arrived over the rail of the boat. They fished it out of the plastic bag and gave it a shake, checking for size and general quality. It didn't seem too bad. It was actually a baggy smock-like thing that she could maybe wear in bed. She rolled it and stuffed it back in the plastic bag as Gerald peered over the side of the boat and nodded. He then placed the mobile firmly in his right hand and with a cricket-type sweep of the arm, launched it into Egypt. It was a clean catch and its new owner seemed impressed. One or two of his compatriots cast a quizzical eye in his direction in an attempt to ascertain the extent of luck that seemed to have come his way.

It had been quite exhausting shouting things down over the side of the boat like that and it hadn't been easy because the men's English was so bad. It was time to relax with a cup of tea. They eased themselves into the chairs reassuring themselves first that the seats were stable and that their hats were appropriately angled against the sun. Meryl seemed pleased with her purchase and there could be no complaints. A mobile phone, albeit old and not working properly, wasn't a bad swap for a top that you wore in bed. But the point was re-iterated that if the men intended to make money, they must learn to speak English properly. They applied dollops of cream to their faces and laid back in their chairs squinting their eyes against the light as they tilted their faces to the sun. A handful of buzzards continued to circle animatedly above them.

Time and the banks of the Nile passed slowly by. Some of the cruisers stood in a line leaning against the rail passively observing the yellows greens and palms with their occasional settlements and homes cut out of the earth that bordered the water. From the river bank their heads appeared small; distant – silhouetted against the sun like punctuation marks. Children splashing in pools or labouring under clumps of timber or younger brothers and sisters, waved and shouted as the cruisers gently waved their arms to and fro back at them – like a valedictory scene on the wave of a previous decade.

Meryl and Gerald lay on their bed, arms folded across their midriffs; soft ripples of lips from exhaling air, hall-marks of the daily ritual of afternoon sleep. Gerald's head lay slightly angled, a small trickle of saliva slipping onto the sheet from the corner of his mouth. The newspaper lay between them, folded open at the crossword page. They'd managed most of it; twenty one across was causing them problems and seventeen down. They'd ask Tom and Alice later.

After about ten minutes, Gerald came round and blinked a few times to get his bearings. He rose a little on his elbows and gazed out of a port-hole. The boat was passing one of the first temples to have been hewn from the huge banks of clay – still complete with internal chambers and interwoven passages. He turned back to the cabin and reached for a custard-cream biscuit in the packet at the side of the bed. Sitting up he crunched the biscuit with a slow rhythmic motion of his jaws, cupping a hand underneath to catch the crumbs. He turned again to twenty-one across, and then lay down, on his other side this time. And soon the cabin fell back into silence, apart from his snores.

Late evening stretched across the skies in strands of apricot broken with streaks of deep blues, greens and mauves, as Meryl and Gerald emerged, slightly awkwardly, through the cabin door into the corridor. They made their way to the Rameses bar where, after earlier deliberation, they'd agreed to meet Tom and Alice at eight-forty five which gave them time after dinner to relax and let their evening meal go down and then get ready for the evening. There was no point in rushing; that was the idea of a cruise – you took your time about things. Meryl's shoes were biting a bit in the heel because they were new – the leather hadn't quite softened enough yet. She was hobbling a little and Gerald asked her if she was okay. She said 'yes', it was just the shoes that were biting a bit. They stopped while he had a look and hooked his finger round the leather to try to pull it a bit. She put it back on and hobbled a bit further, hanging on to her husband a little more tightly than usual.

By the time they arrived, the bar was busy and the piano was in full swing. They met Tom and Alice, both of whom were concerned to hear about Meryl's shoe. Tom said they should hit it with a hammer. But they didn't have a hammer. Maybe one of the waiters could get one. They'd ask later. They ordered drinks – Meryl was going to take it easy on the Bacardi and Cokes after all that sun. Tom fancied a gin and tonic for a change. He was usually a whisky-man, but he found a gin and tonic refreshing on occasions, particularly with ice and a slice of lemon. Alice ordered half a lager shandy; she was feeling a bit thirsty. Gerald ordered a pint of Boddingtons.

They managed to get four places, though it took some manoeuvring, getting themselves down into those low squashy seats. You had to put your hands on the arms and kind of ease yourself down into them. Why the seats weren't a little higher was a mystery. But never mind. They were there now and at least they'd got seats. The clock showed that 'The Night Of The Pharaohs' would be starting soon. Gerald hadn't been serious about dressing as a pharaoh or Cleopatra and Meryl's shoe was still hurting. Alice and Tom were discussing about whether to go for the 'cocktail of the day' next. Gerald took the newspaper and asked them if they had any idea of twenty-one across. They weren't sure; they'd thought it might be 'pinnacle', but that meant eleven across was wrong - 'aroma' - and they didn't see what else that could be. They decided to abandon it for the day. There was always tomorrow's. Instead they sat back and listened to the piano.

One of the Philippinos came over to check that everyone was happy. They said 'yes' but asked him if he had a hammer. He asked why they wanted a hammer and Meryl showed him her shoe. He said he'd see what he could do. Outside – in Egypt – the sun and buzzards had finally disappeared, taking a well-earned break. On the boat, things were starting to liven up; 'The Night Of The Pharaohs' was about to begin.

# The Plaque Carrier

Sigmund Hefnick trudged the next few steps of his weary route across the ramshackle salt-beds and stony tyre-tracks – a terrain that had barely changed since the year dot and had been his people's home for some several hundred years and more.

The sun flared like a million coal fires, his legs ached and his arms pulled wearily at their sockets under the weight of his knapsack, the plaques and the day-to-day survival kit that a mission such as his demanded.

He took a moment to peer into the blinding sky, wipe a few strains of sweat from his forehead and check with his watch. There were still some eight miles to be covered before his schedule could allow him to take respite and set about his victuals and call it a day. He tipped a measured glug of his 'Mountain Spring Water' down his throat and set off once more, pacing himself across the hard-baked earth that would take him eventually to his next port of call.

He was tiring quickly and on more than one occasion stopped in his tracks, distracted by what appeared to be conglomerations of grape-vines and olive-groves shimmering under the heat, but which, on closer investigation, proved to be just another of the weird, twisted hallucinations that, in these parts, sent many a man to a premature grave in a fit of despair and delirium.

It was getting hotter and his path was not an easy one – taking him, as it did, across one of the bleakest environments on earth. His thirst was ceaseless and he found himself forced to rest at least every half-hour.

Sigmund Hefnick was a man on a mission.

The country was going to the dogs (and had been for some time.) Sin was rife: the cities – once monuments to unquestioning subservience reduced to little more than labyrinthine dens of licentiousness and greed: nose-jobs at ten-a-penny, silicon implants, plastic refurbishments...all for a quick buck in seedy recesses of back-street cubicles and rat-infested alleyways, whilst buses hurtled round corners bearing the scurrilous claim ... *'There might not be a God – It's official...!'*
The 'Sick Man Of The East' was indeed 'sick'!

It was all too much for the men in grey smocks who promptly summoned themselves to the sanctuary of the Council House, where – after much soul-searching and recrimination – the 'facts' (a plain and unadulterated exposition of their plight) would be laid bare before the public.There could be only one solution: a one-way ticket en-route to a Better Tomorrow. They must – in short – get 'Back To Basics'. A return to the fundamental ideology that had been the building block of their universe since time immemorial. 'The Truth, The Whole Truth, and Nothing But The Truth –would be the mantra seen flying once more from every town-centre flagpole the length and breadth of the land.

And – there would be no pussy-footing around – no dissenters.; there'd been too much of that in the past. Wavering voices – such as they were – would be summarily whipped into submission and nailed to the gatepost; an example of what can be achieved with a little discipline and a gentle push in the right direction.

And so it came to pass that Sigmund Hefnick, a lower ranking minion of the local Elders, found himself bestowed with the honour of travelling the length and breadth of the land, taking time out at each and every township, where he would nail a plaque – deliberately scrawled in huge letters for the benefit of the nation's illiterate majority – to the whipping posts in the market-place – to be seen by all and serve as a firm reminder of just what lay in store for anyone foolish enough to be found wallowing around in a vice-ridden, godless world, devoid of meaning or purpose.

It was with his eight miles finally behind him, that Sigmund finally took his 'snap' from his knapsack and his goats' milk from his flask to take respite amongst the sheep and donkeys that were the mainstay of a man's company in these parts. For convenience, he pitched his plaques in the sand and settled himself in their midst, to partake of his evening's victuals and dig himself a little hole, where – within a matter of minutes – he would be lost to the world.

Which was unfortunate. Or, more precisely, it was unfortunate that he had seen fit to leave the plaques in the public gaze, for his decision had, unwittingly, failed to take into account, the arrival of one Gaelfric Haelbetyouone – a simple-minded peasant, who, en-route to his homestead after a hard day's graft in the fields, was somewhat surprised to come across an array of signs stuck in the sand, and in their midst, their bearer, slumped fast asleep.

Now whilst Gaelfric Haelbetyouone was not of first-rate intelligence – in fact he was completely stupid – he was a loyal and obedient servant who always took heed to be respectful of his Elders and Betters.

And thus, on arrival at the sleeping man's side, he immediately took it upon himself to take note of the wording on the plaques that the man had displayed around him, for a quick glance at the man's garb was enough to convince him that he was quite likely a minion of the Elders and most certainly one of his Betters.

It was no easy task, but, with the aid of a finger, he worked his way painstakingly along the lines, until he finally drew a hand to his mouth and gasped.

For there on each and every plaque – clearly visible under the beacon of soft, silvery moonlight.....were the plain, unadulterated facts.......

> *Punishments for a man found 'loafing around' in a Godless world:*
>
> *Removal of tongue......for he has nothing worth saying*
> *Removal of eyes......for he is blind to the truth*
> *Removal of ears......for he is deaf to it too*
>
> *Removal of hands......for he reaches for*
> *nothing beyond the spoils of*
> *wickedness and vice*
> *There can be no exceptions......It has been decreed......*
> *from above...*

It took young Gaelfric some time to come to terms with the enormity – and length – of such words. But, after several re-readings, the 'facts' were there, staring him full in the face: this cat's-whisker – this jackass – lying there humped under the moonlight, sleeping the sleep of babes, was clearly a heathen – an infidel who – having finally seen the errors of his ways had pitched himself in the sand, in readiness to receive his just deserts.

Young Gaelfric cast an eye across the desert wasteland, and set about doing some thinking. There was clearly justice to be done and no sense to be drawn in its delay.

Drawing himself to full height he raised an eye to the heavens. For what was equally clear, was that he – Gaelfric Haelbetyouone – a simple peasant from a shack of mud-daub and corrugated tin – had been blessed; blessed with the task of 'righting wrong'....in doing his bit for 'good' to triumph over 'evil'.

He was, at once, filled with such pride, he could barely think straight.

But, there was no time for dillying and dallying. There was work to be done. For while the man was evidently a philanderer – a monkey-spanker – he was not, as yet, without his aforesaid 'bits', for there they were, sitting, as proud as punch, still attached to the rest of him.

There must be no delay. For who could say the man, currently lying there semi-comatosed to the world, wouldn't, at any moment, rise from his sojourn to wreak yet more havoc on their new-found God-fearing way of life?

He reached to his waist. It was fortunate that – in these days of soaring crime-rates – he always carried a razor-sharp knife.

He withdrew the weapon, feasting his eyes on the gleaming, twinkling blade. The question was, where to start? Should he work his way down or up? He decided to start with the tongue, for that would, at least put paid to him mouthing any more of his nonsense, and then the eyes – for what use has a man for eyes if he cannot see? Then, the ears – silence would indeed be golden as far as this chap was concerned, and…finally, the hands…..let him, from hereon reach for nothing 'cept his missing bits that would have been swept away by the winds of the desert by now.

With beating heart and resolution of spirit, he moved in. He knew he must be quick, for guilty men had a habit of kicking up a fuss about these things, even with their guilt surrounding them from all angles.

He took a deep breath and in a single move, reached into the sleeping man's mouth, seizing the tongue between thumb and forefinger. He yanked it forwards and with a swift slice of the blade, removed it near the root. He looked down to inspect a two-and-a-half inch lump dangling from his fingers and a small scarlet fountain pumping from between the man's teeth.

Time was precious and, ignoring the man's protests and gesticulations, he quickly hooked the point of the blade above an eye and with a flick of the wrist, flopped the gelatinous glob from its comfort-zone to halfway down his cheek. He repeated the process on the other side and flicked the two jelly-balls into a nearby ditch to turn his attention to the ears. A couple more slices and the wrinkly digits were promptly whipped from their base. He turned, spiking the pair on a nearby cactus plant; a treat for the buzzards when the breakfast bell tolled. And finally, the hands. Taking one and holding it against the other, he sliced his way through the pair, watching as the two digits dropped to the dust, their stumps coiling and quivering like a couple of red-leafed palm-trees.

Job done; the chap was finally on the road to redemption.

He wiped the blade with the lower skirts of his tunic and replaced the knife in its sheaf at his waist. Standing to make his departure, he glanced down at the figure moaning and whining in the dust: a man clearly beside himself with guilt and remorse.

But, young Gaelfric wasn't yet done! As he popped the blade back in its scabbard, there were vague stirrings at the back of his mind – vague recollections trailing back to his schooldays; something along the lines of *rewards* for doing good and vanquishing evil...or was it *gifts*? Something about 'Salvation In The Garden Of Paradise' rang a few bells.

Anyway, the bottom line was, having done his bit for *A Better Tomorrow*, there was every chance there might be something in it for him, just as long as he was able to produce the evidence.

So, with thumping heart and visions of some future paradise waiting in the wings, he grabbed the squirming body and heaved it, belly-up, over his ass. The next town was some twenty miles to the north; there was no time to waste.

It was a slow plodding journey. The ass was well into its doting years and its load slumped across its back was no meagre weight. It was around tea-time the following day that he finally dragged his critter along the dust-path that led to the nearest House Of The Elders. His passenger, who had been gurgling away to himself for most of the trip, had taken to flailing his stumps in the air in an attempt to get some attention from the plethora of basket-weavers and market sellers. But people in these parts knew better than to have their attention drawn to strangers twitching and gesticulating from the back of an ass.

They finally came to a halt outside a palatial castle – a huge thing, the turrets of which reared into the sky in an indescribable display of ugliness. Gaelfric was quite overcome by it all and repeatedly pinched himself to confirm that he wasn't in the middle of some crazy reverie; that he – Gaelfric Haelbetyouone – a simple peasant from a pile of mud-daub and corrugated tin – was, at this moment, standing in the midst of unimaginable opulence and grandeur.

As instructed at the gate, he drew his ass to a standstill and waited for the arrival of a Chief Elder. Meanwhile, he looked down to see how his man was faring. He had barely moved over the last two miles or so – probably exhausted by the crushing heat.

Moments later, a man appeared – a big-bellied, fearsome-looking figure with eyes like crows' feet. He checked out the scene and sniffed a few times in the air, musing as to how this lack-lustre peasant and his irksome-looking load could possibly concern him at this hour of the day.

'What's this then?' he asked, speaking in a deep, stentorian tone. Gaelfric wasn't quite sure of the answer he should give, so he grinned and nodded down at the rapidly wilting ass and its burden lying across its midriff.

The man took a few steps closer, trying to make some sense of the strange gurgling sounds coming from the other side of the donkey's back, but making little of it. 'Friend of yours?' he asked, walking round to check the scene from a different angle. Gaelfric shook his head but again, said nothing. Truth be told, he was more than a little intimidated by men who resided in huge palaces and felt it might be politic to keep communication with him to a bare minimum.

Instead, he made his way to the ass's rear quarters where he unhooked a leather satchel and withdrew one of the plaques the man had posted around him in the desert. (For convenience, he had decided to leave most of them where he had found them.) He held it up – pointing a finger at the words printed on the flat, white background and then at the man dangling over the ass.

The Elder read the words and cast an eye over the figure still twitching and gurgling beneath him. He took a few steps forward, tapping his lip. There was something about the man's garb that seemed familiar; it was the kind of smock worn by some of their lower-ranking minions.

'Hmm,' he said, stroking his chin and taking a quick glance at Gaelfric, who had taken to hopping from foot to foot, quite awe-struck at being in the presence of a man of such disposition and standing.

It was at the third circumambulation of the ass that the man stopped and smiled to himself.

The facts were clear: the sad man had – almost literally – grabbed the wrong end of the stick – a cut-and-dried case of mistaken-identity; an easy mistake to make in these days of mass ignorance and superstition.

The Elder looked across at the sundial waning rapidly in the thickening hours of evening and set about some serious thinking. He cast his eyes around the courtyard. There were no signs of life – just a few banks of shuttered windows and abandoned doorways; beyond that, nothing; just the three of them – four if you counted the ass.

There was no escaping the facts – for 'facts' were relevant, and not so stupid or indeed irrelevant as some might claim. And the 'facts' here were very plain. The hapless fellow had put two and two together, made five, and in so doing, had – albeit inadvertently – taken the most precious gifts of a man's limbs.

Still, no worries....these things happen.

The Elder looked upward to the skies and then to the man stood before him, still hopping from foot to foot, in wide-eyed expectation of what was about to befall him.

There was clearly justice to be done and no sense to be drawn in its delay.

'Sir, you have done good work,' said The Elder, raising an arm in celebration of the man's feat.

'Thankyou sir....thankyou.....thankyou...,' replied Gaelfric – near speechless in anticipation of the fortune that was surely about to drop into his lap.

'And accordingly, it falls to me to lead us both in a simple act of contrition. You will raise your head skywards and in time-honoured tradition, I shall lay The Gift Of Eternal Life....upon your shoulders.'

'Thankyou sir – thankyou...' said Gaelfric, raising his eyes in acknowledgement of the man's words and future sanctuary in the upper echelons.

At which point, The Elder, taking a razor-sharp knife from the scabbard at his side, administered a well-aimed slice – sending the aforesaid head tumbling into the dust, and a magnificent fountain of scarlet cascading toward the heavens, where it hung like a bouquet of fine wine – before descending to earth to form thick pools around the smiling face peering up at him from the dirt.

The Elder replaced his weapon and looked down. He couldn't help but feel some sympathy as he dumped young Gaelfric over Sigmund, giving his head a hefty boot in the process to send it scuttling across the courtyard into the bushes where it would, at least temporarily, lie concealed from vision.

He turned a grateful eye to the skies. The country – it seemed – was finally on the mend.

# Home Abroad

## ONE

Billy Longstaffe eased himself into his customary reclining position on his plastic chair. His porky legs stretched out – feet apart, heels barely touching the baking tiles of the veranda; head reclined in glorious supplication to the sky. He twitched occasionally when a midge or mosquito invaded his space and then he'd turn left or right to try to locate the offending critter and then sink back into quiet repose. All was well with his world; there was little to do, little to be done and all the time in the world to do it. His arms folded over his belly which had flourished these days to an impressive overhang and in horizontal recline, thick folds of flesh rippled under his exhalations and a warm basting of oily sweat. Doctors would probably advise he should shed a few stone, but he rarely went to the doctor's and was more than happy to haul his pile of belly around, taking pride in the way it jiggled and rolled whenever he stirred himself to go to the bathroom or kitchen for a beer. To him it was a fine belly and a decent girth gave a man a 'presence', a 'stature', an air of self-confidence, unlike those puny individuals that you sometimes saw, particularly back in the UK.

His wife was faffing about with some potted plant that she couldn't decide where to stick on the patio. In contrast to her husband, she was lean and scrawny, like a large underfed rook. Age had eaten away at her with little sympathy, leaving folds of parchment-like skin hanging off her bones in long turkey-like pouches. She wore a limp, listless expression with thin drawn lips, whose main task was to hold a Rothmans Kingsize for most of her waking hours.

Their habitat was one of many 'urbanisations'of whitewashed housing projects that in recent years had come to spread from the peripheries of many of the towns of the area into the shoulders and valleys of mountainsides, stretching to the length and breadth of the southern Spanish coastline. A large number of the inhabitants were ex-pat Brits who, having savoured a few summers in the sun, had taken the plunge in seeking colonisation of these more affable climes.

It got particularly hot at that time of day – early to mid afternoon when the sun unleashed itself in full glory on the patios, walls and tiny lanes. Rivulets of sweat rolled over Billy's torso, settling in his belly area folds and dripping down his eyelids. This was the life. This was what it was all about.

His wife stood behind him in the lounge nursing a gin and tonic and drawing on the fag that hung from her lips like a spare limb. For her the afternoons could get a little too much. And for those few hours she would seek the relief of the living room or nearby bar. On this particular afternoon, she fancied the bar. Norma and Jim would probably be there and Alec and Rose as like as not. They could maybe take in a bite to eat, save having to switch the cooker on.

She approached the patio and stared out through her exhaled cloud of smoke at the mountains – grey and jagged – swathed in a kind of ethereal haze in the afternoon sun. Beneath the mountains lay long brown and greyish green stretches of low-lying allotment patches, scrubland, plastic-covered tomato tents, vine clumps, dotted restaurants and a patchwork of tiny white settlements and villas. She took another drag and flicked the ash.

'Bill...Fancy Ka Ka's?' she asked, in her customary desultory tone of voice. There was no immediate answer. Bill was lost enough to the sun-god to feel any need to talk to his wife at that particular moment. She stood a little longer and took another drag.

'What d'you reckon? I'm getting a bit bored.' She was leaning against the door jamb morosely scratching a midge bite somewhere down by her left rib.

He grunted and chopped his lips to destroy the lines of sweat that were trickling into his mouth.

'Well fuck it then, I'll go on my own,' she said with an edge of irritation, stubbing out a third of the remainder of the Rothmans and blowing the last of the smoke into the air.

'Alright, I'm coming,' said Billy, loathe to display any visible signs of energy at this time of day, particularly to his wife. This was Spain, for fuck's sake. 'Just 'ang on a minute.'

Ka Ka's was the local bar, well patronised by the local residents, most of whom displayed little urge to venture too far beyond its periphery; it was indeed to everyone's benefit that the bar was located where it was – for further down the hill, or somewhere along the main road, would have been off limits and far too great a hassle to consider. As it was, they could drop off the step of their paths and pop almost immediately through the swing doors and into the bar in a few simple movements and not much more than a handful of steps.

Billy and his belly and Edna and her fag clicked the trellis door in place and shuffled up the tiled steps to the road, which, like all the lanes and the pathways of the urbanisation, was lined with a procession of huge fleshy leaves, vibrant flowers and reptilian-looking vines overhanging the small white walls. Above them, at varying points and strategically arranged angles on the hillside, villas perched amongst their webs of red-tiled pathways, black garden fencing, rubber plants and more full bloodied flowers and orange trees stretching to the upper reaches of the hill and beyond.

Edna flicked her ash and swore at a small stone that had found its way into her flip-flop. Billy, breathing heavily from the exertions of movement, contemplated his belly folds and wiped the sweat from his brow whilst he waited for her to finish hobbling around on one leg, shaking her foot.

It was a good eighty or ninety yards to the bar, but they finally made it and shoved its entrance doors apart.

Two English couples were already seated at the bar, smoking and occasionally reaching for gin and tonics that sat on the bar top. Alec and Rose had moved from Bedford some two or three years ago and Norma and Jim were longer standing residents, having moved from Corby about five years previously. The bar was part of an overall complex, labelled 'La Palma' – a geometrically designed arrangement of tiny lawns and pathways, complete with thatched shades, shielded plastic tables and sun-beds.

A poolside kiosk delivered Cokes, toasted sarnis or egg and chips, courtesy of the long-suffering waiter Miguel, a taciturn, sour-looking individual, who had little time for the pleasantries some felt his job ought to embrace, but whose commitment to the business, whether pulling pints or beavering away behind the scene and beer crates in the shed-like kitchen in temperatures of near a hundred degrees, could never be questioned.

The bar's interior had a loosely patriotic air with beer mat displays, English brewery logo'd mirrors, photos of currently in-vogue footballers and a pile of yesterday's Sun, Mirror or Star, enabling the punters to keep well up with their reading.

They acknowledged each other and Billy ordered his pint of Boddingtons from Micky, the bar owner, a gruff-talking scouser and divorcee who'd arrived from England about eighteen months ago, having bought the business off a fellow called Tom from Huddersfield. Micky certainly kept the place better stocked than Tom had tended to do and in addition, had a lucrative sideline in cut-price fags, courtesy of some business contacts in Malaga.

Edna took a seat on a bar stool, but was far from happy. 'Bleeding stone,' she grumbled, still unable to shake off the offending article for some reason. She placed her fag in the ash tray and removed the flip flop to give it a resounding wallop against the bar top, making Jim – who had been keeping half an eye on the golf on Sky – but had started to doze off – jump back to life. He tipped the remaining contents of a bag of dry-roasted peanuts in his hand and shovelled them into his mouth, whilst turning his attention back to the Sky screen. His wife had stayed back in the villa, she'd been feeling knackered all day – probably the heat.

Temperatures in the bar were kept to a mostly bearable level by a thatched roof stretching to some twenty, thirty feet from the bar itself and a number of fans strategically placed next to the crisps and ice cream freezer. The regulars always took their places on the stools in a line at the bar, elbows propped on the bar, facing the walls – a formation that successfully restricted conversation to occasional grunts. They mostly had little to say to each other and more than enough time to be saying it.

Alec, the youngest of them, was giving Jim a blow-by-blow account of his latest conquest in town. He was a stringy looking individual approaching middle-age with a superbly coiffed pony-tail of grey hair. He broke with convention by making regular forays into the nearby town, where he liked to fraternise with the local waiters, perceiving his 'chumminess' with them as evidence of his 'Spanishness' and an integral part of his de-anglicisation. Most of the waiters, obliged to suffer his inane lines of banter thought he was a prat, but as many a waiter will tell you, delivering plates to tables is only part of the job when the more demanding punter comes along seeking pretences of fondness and affability.

And in addition to that, being in town gave him the opportunity to get his hands on as many women as possible (there were more of them in town) as he had been bored with his wife – particularly in bed – for about the last fifteen years. Fortunately his wife held him in comparable esteem and levelled the scales by leaping into the sack with as many males as she could get to join her in it.

Micky's bar catered ideally for the Spanish way of life – Skol lager and Boddington's bitter on tap, the Sky box for their Premiership football and full English breakfasts, burger and chips and Sunday lunches. In fact, just how they'd managed to stick it out in England for as long as they had, was something of a mystery and a recurrent topic of conversation. They would often take their turns in reminding each other – lest any of them should have forgotten – just what a crappy place England was, and run over once again just what it was that had prompted them to find a new life in Spain. On that particular afternoon it was Jim's turn to remind them that England was a grey place, inhabited by grey people doing grey things in a grey climate. Add - the prices, 'nanny state' politicians; and of course, when we say England, do we mean 'England', or are we talking about a foreign enclave for asylum-seekers and black and Asian ghettoes?'

'You wouldn't catch me going back there,' said Bill.

'What's the point? What is there in England? Someone tell me,' said Alec, sipping his lager and flicking open his copy of The Sun for a quick shufty at page three and making a quick comparison with his misses.

'Grey people and grey days,' said Clive, who had been half sharing the conversation over his pint and a game of darts with Ken.

Miguel suddenly appeared from the kitchen, bearing plates of sausage and chips and looking a bit flustered. Things had been getting a bit hectic round the pool area – there'd been an influx of customers. Word had gone around that jellyfish had been spotted in the sea. In these parts jellyfish were no laughing matter – despite the name. A jellyfish could wrap itself round you and cling like a vice, doing you serious damage in the process; unless you happened to be a bar owner in their vicinity.

On the day in question the red flags were out and a number of punters had decided to cut their losses, grab their towels, lotions and paperbacks and plod their way in retreat through the grey mud coloured sand to the sanctuary of the bars.

Miguel wasn't necessarily complaining, far from it – but he was looking a bit flustered. Fortunately his wife helped out in the season, though she tended to keep herself almost permanently out of sight in the kitchen – an arrangement that appeared to meet their mutual approval.

Norman arrived. He was an elderly resident who had just been playing petanque. He remarked on how the sea had emptied – a weird sight in July and August and it was apparently because of jellyfish. They told him they'd heard, and flicked their heads in the general direction of the influx of customers. Norman's calling-card was an endless delivery of poor, to moderately poor, jokes, of a predictably dubious nature.

As he looked around for a vacant stool he told them how his wife had once been stung by a jellyfish, but it had survived. They'd had this one a few times but, ironically enough, it had actually happened. It had occurred one day last Summer. The sting had been high on her thigh, which had irritated Norman no end. He would have much preferred it to have been somewhere up near the middle of her back, or maybe on her foot, or maybe across her face which would have kept her indoors and out of action for a week or two, but not up the top of her leg, for Christ's sake. Norman's drinking habits were a little unusual in that he drank his red wine chilled; sometimes with ice and soda.

He took his place at the bar complaining about the weather and noisy kids and the shirt sticking to his back. Whose idea it was to play petanque in the afternoon in August he couldn't begin to fathom. He ordered his wine from the fridge as Miguel emerged from the back in a bit of a rush and still looking a bit flustered.

Alec, who'd been pre-occupied down at the poolside attempting to get on familiar terms with two adolescent schoolgirls from Hoylake hadn't yet spotted Miguel.

As he emerged from behind the bar he made his move with an outstretched arm and a smile.

'Miguel my friend,' he said, placing the arm convivially around his shoulder and tapping him gently on the upper arm. Miguel acknowledged him, but with little enthusiasm – he had work to do, unlike these idle English sods.

## TWO

The doors opened and two couples in their mid-twenties entered and cast their eyes quickly round the bar's interior, spotting that there were tables free. Sounding a bit like a nursery rhyme, they were Colin and Mandy, Steve and Sandy and though their visit to Spain was part holiday, they were looking to buy a place they were hoping to convert into a new bar with all the trimmings. Although only recent arrivals – from about four days ago – extended sessions under the sun had already got them to the stage where they could look in the mirror with some pride, assured that they were well on the way to achieving their target of turning to the colour of a chair leg; and thus close to casting off that most unwanted vestige of new arrivals from England – looking like you come from England. As they made their way to a table they noticed with some satisfaction just how the subdued light of the bar made them look so incredibly tanned.

Having seated themselves round the table they made playful grabs for the one and only menu that stood in the centre. They were in exuberant mood, full of hope about the properties that Antonio had earmarked for them. They put their bags down and Steve reached for the map that was stuffed between the Factor Ten and his Dan Brown novel. Steve spent a fair amount of time with maps, not so much reading them, but more trying to get them into shape. It always took a while to negotiate the bit he wanted and then the folds always refused to fold and it tended to stick out like a concertina'd fan. After a few attempts he swore at it and plonked it down on the table, leaning across it to try and flatten it with his arm. Sandy watched him with feigned dismay and a roll of her eyes.

'Honestly you're so useless,' she said, taking the map and organising it methodically and orderly and then placing it down neatly and correctly opened in front of him. 'See, just a little patience; just a little female intuition. It isn't rocket science.' He swore at her and set about trying to find the place with his finger.

It took some time to be served, as Miguel was being rushed off his feet but they didn't mind – there was no rush – this was Spain after all. Eventually they got round to placing their order for bottled San Miguels, mineral water and red wine (la casa.) Two of them bent their heads over the map, their fingers tracing little patterns over the area nearby until eventually finding a place that could be the place Antonio had mentioned – it sounded right; though Colin wasn't so sure, didn't it begin with 'O'? Mandy and Sandy thought not. They took out the slip of paper to check. That was it – that was the place – it was where Antonio had said, near the mountains and about two Ks off the main road.

The place in question was a small village set in the cradle of the nearby mountains. By virtue of its relative isolation, it had remained almost untouched and unblemished by the nation's recent economic revolution, but in the recent upsurge in demand for a more 'rustic' setting, now lay – like a defenceless creature - ripe for picking in the hands of any number of property marketeers, with an eye on a quick and hefty profit. The village was, as Sandy had put it when they had first seen the photos in the office in town.... 'absolutely amazing' - its small homes and dusty street embodying everything one might imagine of a Spain from a bygone age. So now was the time to move in.

Antonio was an integral part in the whole operation; a snappy looking fellow with dark features, four languages and a penchant for light coloured suits. He had always had his sights fixed firmly on his financial future and as a number of initial ventures in Home Improvement and DIY had folded, he'd quickly become aware of the most lucrative route to success. Both Carol and Sandy thought he was 'amazing' and he had certainly made it his habit to be pleasant and courteous to his customers – or more specifically, the ones from abroad with money in the bank and the purchase of property on their minds. His magnanimity was somewhat less in evidence in his dealings with his own countrymen, particularly those whose businesses crossed his own in what he perceived to be a less than business-like approach. But, this was Spain and there were compensatory factors: one of which, was the potential for quick and substantial profits in the purchase and sale of older properties located out of town, though there'd been occasions when he'd have happily exchanged a significant percentage of profit for a drainpipe or electric fuse box being fitted without the delays and convoluted wrangles that such procedures often seemed to involve.

Having eventually found the office from the ad in the town's weekly magazine, the four of them had poured their heads over the table as Antonio opened the folder of A4 polythene sleeves to reveal back-to-back bold clean photographic displays of various properties currently 'up for grabs' in the vicinity, whilst offering encouraging explanations of just how each might well come pretty close to realising their needs. Many of them were quiet, abandoned-looking places, completely unspoilt and certainly at the cheaper end of the market, which was the area they were targeting in order to restore the place in the style that they had in mind And of course there was the huge 'plus' of such places not being in the least 'touristy' - which were the last sort of places you wanted to settle in.

Together they leafed through the possibilities, finally settling on two that seemed to fit the bill. Certainly there would be considerable work to be done, but that was the idea, if they were to fulfil their ambitions and realise their dreams.

With an air of anticipation they had arranged to meet Antonio late the following afternoon at the tiny village that none of them had the slightest inkling of, other than it was there – listed in black and white (and colour) under the polythene sheet.

It was about seven-o-clock the following evening and a few miles out of Condorisma, that their car abandoned the neat tarmac of the 'A' road to turn into a small lane formed mainly of dust and tire tracks in the earth, flanked by sharp and dying bushes, rusting pipes and the odd broken concrete wall or hut. Beyond them expanses of empty groves reached to dotted homesteads and the gentle inclines of the lower mountains.

Their only company in these parts were occasional carts hauled along by donkeys, their weary expressions drawn from lives of uncompromising hardship. And at their sides, small men in straw hats and hanging shirts - their legs, spindly as their donkeys, hooded in flapping trousers – walking in slow-paced sympathy with their animals' knock-kneed movements.

It was another kilometre or so before the lane led its way to the first ramshackle sheds and walls of the village, leading to the main street where small houses stretched the length of the street like a line of ageing whitewashed molars.

At the roadside, adjoining a longish wooden fenced patio was a tiny bar terrace where a handful of men, unkempt and unshaven, with faces like wallnuts, were seated for the daily ritual of dominos or cards. On the table before them stood grubby little glasses of some unidentifiable liquid the colour of nicotine tar.

At the whirr of the car engine, battered old caps perked up and faces turned to observe the commotion – the cards or dominoes temporarily forgotten.

Their eyes remained fixed on the car and its occupants, as the doors were flung open spilling the last throes of Elton John's 'Goodbye Yellow Brick Road' CD into the late afternoon air.

Mandy and Sandy had already fallen in love with the place, so simple and unspoilt as it was, and Colin and Steve's initial impression was that it was 'absolutely amazing'. The four of them climbed out of the car and breathed in the surroundings, looking over at the terrace bar.

'Hi,' Mandy shouted warmly and waving, her light cotton skirt skipping round her thighs.

'Yo,' added Colin, standing and straightening his 'Hard Rock Café' tee-shirt which had wrinkled from sitting in the back of the vehicle.

There was no response from the veranda, where the men continued to stare, their eyes as sharp as flint in the rough leathery features around them. A few lean-looking cats on stilt-like legs, drew themselves from under the table to keep their own eye on proceedings.

The car doors were slammed shut and the central-locking applied. And for a moment, the four of them stood, savouring the rustic ambience of what could potentially be their new home. Eventually Sandy made a step towards the bar terrace and pointed up the lane.

'We're looking at a place up near the top of the road,' she said, still pointing and speaking deliberately slowly and clearly, mindful that you couldn't be sure just how much English people in places like this actually spoke or understood. Steve approached to lend his support.

'We like the village,' he said, also speaking with exaggerated clarity. 'It's absolutely amazing.' He fixed his eyes on the men as he spoke, aware that a few seeds of friendship could be sewn here with them being potentially new neighbours. Their gestures drew only stares, that continued to fix on them in unblinking silence.

Mandy approached the terrace, her attention caught by the cats, all of which had continued to study them with the same curiosity as their menfolk. She adored cats.

'Hello,' she said, playfully leaning forward to one of them and rubbing her forefinger and thumb together, as if offering some tit-bit as a friendly gesture. The cats eased their necks forward in mild curiosity and one even took a step towards her as if sensing there might be something on offer.

The four engaged in a few private verbal exchanges and took a few glances up the street whilst checking with their watches. It was close to the time they had agreed to meet Antonio and it might be best to make their way to find the agreed rendezvous point. With a wave to the guys they headed off.

'We might be moving in. We've come to view property,' said Colin, feeling that some explanation for their presence might be in order. 'We're from England,' he added finally. And with that they turned to focus their attention on the lane ahead and the stones under their feet.

The locals could have been excused for thinking some full-scale invasion was imminent when, before time had lapsed to raise glasses to lips, a second car whirled out of oblivion and came hurtling onto the scene in front of them. Antonio was no slouch when it came to driving his car, and as he skidded his way passed the veranda, a spray of loose dust and stones sent cats scurrying to the security of the wall and drew the men's attention once again into the middle of the street. But almost before heads had turned, Antonio was already sliding to a halt some hundred or so yards further up the road.

Having drawn his car to the appointed spot and stepped out, he acknowledged the others with a wave of the hand and made his way towards them. There is a correct way of doing business and it begins with handshakes. Antonio, looking as sharp and clean as a new knife under the evening sun, was quick to take control and lead them to the property whilst explaining in colourful terms just how he had an inkling this might turn out to be the ideal place for them. And after a brief examination and walk round the building and land's circumference, it seemed that he could well be right. It was ideal – exactly the kind of place they were hoping to find.

The property had formerly been a small-holding for the packing and distribution of olives. It comprised a sturdy looking house with a kitchen suitably located at the front. The front area comprised a large patio that had been used for the tethering of donkeys or packing of boxes or something and a bordering area near a low stone wall. Antonio led them round the outside and inside and after about ten minutes initial plans were already starting to take shape. Included in the 'deal' was a small adjacent building which had been used as a storage area. It presently lay derelict and was littered with the remnants of boxes and bits of old carpet. Steve did a quick inspection and was convinced it could be converted without too much fuss and expense into an internet-café and mobile phone outlet.

Back at the main property, the large forecourt would be the main bar area – big enough to accommodate a dance floor and surrounding tables and chairs. Above head-height, a series of grapevines intricately woven in looping shapes around overhanging branches could easily be ripped out and replaced by bright neon lights in flashing time-sequenced circuits running round the entire perimeter of the dance floor – ideal for special 'disco' and 'party' nights. Their excitement grew by the second, particularly when Antonio, concurring with their vision, quickly pointed out other subtle little touches that could enhance the project even further.

He walked them round down the side of the wall to an annexe that had formerly been an olive store, or something like that, but which would be just about big enough for a Mini Sports Bar, complete with Sky satellite dish and a hatch that could be built into the far wall to deliver burgers and fries.

There were smiles all round. There would be considerable building work to be done, but they had budgeted generously and with some help from a number of sources whose co-operation had already been loosely secured, they could already sense that it was an on-going proposition. Ideally they'd need a large neon-lit sign to attract attention from some distance; with maybe something along the lines of ...*Colin & Mandy, Steve & Sandy, Welcome You To* ...on it. They hadn't got as far as the actual name of the place as yet, but would certainly come up with something suitably 'racy' and eye-catching. The question of living space was the only possible problem – but they'd already done some provisional measurements on the three large rooms upstairs and hopefully they'd suffice.

With all the excitement the four of them took time out to sit on the forecourt wall and draw breath to try and take it all in as they cast their eyes over the property and its surroundings. And with not a tourist, or evidence of tourists in sight, it was 'absolutely amazing'.

There was a second possibility that lay in another village about three or four kilometres away, but Antonio was adamant that it no way came as close to meeting their requirements and they'd do themselves a massive favour by committing themselves right there and then to the place in which they were standing. They could see his point. It didn't do to let the grass grow under your feet so to speak – not in these circumstances – this was Spain after all. But it doesn't do to rush these things either, particularly when you're about to change the course of your life.

It was time to retire to the bar down the road. Antonio understood and shook hands and with parting advice about time not standing still, he sped off down the track to attend to other matters, drawing the attention of the guys at the bar for a third time and sending the cats once again to the sanctuary of the bar wall. The four of them, heads together as they walked, made their way down to the bar terrace, where they took seats at the only other table on the veranda.

The men at the other table glanced their way and caught their gazes for a few moments. Colin thought it best to put them in the picture, lest they be curious as to the state-of-play in their speculative venture.

'We're thinking of taking it,' he said, again speaking deliberately slowly and clearly. 'The place up the road. It's amazing. We're going to build a bar; a really good bar – it'll be excellent.'

The news received a few seconds silent attention, but little further reaction. The men returned to their glasses, raising the thick brown liquid to their lips and then as if in some late local ritual, turned their heads and spat, one after the other, in the general direction of the cats perched motionless on stiff giraffe-like legs by the veranda's edge. There was no menu or drinks list at hand, but after various hand gestures and pointing at bits of their 'Travellers' Spanish' book, they hoped they'd managed to order two beers, a wine and a mineral water from a woman in a long black smock, who'd emerged from a back room to see what all the commotion was about.

Questions and more questions were bouncing around in their heads, but whatever uncertainties were voiced, each knew in their heart that they were nothing more than expressions of caution and ten minutes or so later they raised their glasses to drink to their futures in – whatever the place was called – in their excitement they had already forgotten the name. There were issues to be sorted, such as the road to the village; but Antonio had been adamant that permission for building the new road had been granted and preparations were underway for the new surface to be laid in the next few months or so. With parting smiles to the adjacent table they left their seats and plodded across the stones to their car.

It was getting late and the twilight period that seemed to come and go within the space of minutes, had sunk the nearby mountains into jagged black shapes and the street into a deep gloom, broken only by a line of small yellow lights that hung in the air like a fairy grotto. They sighed, taking a wistful look at their future home and then closed the doors, slipped the CD in the slot and drew away from the dim illumination of the bar. The donkeys and carts had disappeared into the hills for the day and the only signs of life were small air-creatures temporarily caught like silver pennants in the car's floodlights.

They hoped Antonio was right about the road building. That was a concern. They needed easier access than this to persuade the punters to get anywhere near the village. A considerable number would obviously be coming from the coast and they might well think twice if they had to bounce around in cars for twenty minutes sloshing bellyfuls of pina-colada around in the process of getting back home.

Soon the car hit the tarmac however and made its less hectic way over the last few kilometres. Tomorrow they'd get to the bank with Antonio and the initial transactions would be completed; at which point the property, back there in – whatever the place was called – would officially be there's.

The road wound its way down to the peripheral parts of town and branched to the right to take them towards Condorisma. The dotted lights of the urbanisation grew closer and even before they eased the car along the driveway to the rented villa, they could hear the beat of the rhythm and volume of sound from Ka Ka's. It was 'Midnight Delight – Disco Night' round the bar and pool area. They parked the car and skipped down the steps to join in, just as 'Rockin' All Over The World' stirred itself to full blast across the surrounding lanes and alleyways.

# The Figure At The Window

Only a slight murmur of conversation could be heard in the classroom and 'a positive atmosphere of learning' prevailed. The teacher, who had returned to his seat to tend to a few things, looked up occasionally to check that everyone was 'on task' and for any hands seeking help or to ask a question. He replaced a few sheets of draft paper into his 'draft paper' box and put the black white-board marking pen in its transparent plastic pencil case. He leant on his elbows for a minute, and then eased back in his chair taking some satisfaction in the scene of activity he had orchestrated. But as ever, after sitting for even a short period, he felt the urge to rise from his chair and walk the aisles to check all was well and watch them occupied with their task.

Today it was a 'Plot-Line' for 'Romeo And Juliet'- one of the GCSE texts, marking in the key points of the lovers' relationship, from the party to the balcony scene, leaving space for further entries as they worked their way through the text in the lessons to come. They'd been asked to draw little arrows labelling the key moments with some examples of quotes from the text. They were allowed to use colour – the girls loved putting bits of colour into their work – though he'd told them not to overdo it or use too heavy felts, which quite frankly, made it look a mess.

He walked slowly down each aisle, watching them draw their little lines in fine-liners and pencils and then exchange them for pens to write the words. One or two asked if they could include pictures and he'd said 'yes of course' if they liked. Samantha (one of the *three* Samantha's, which made life very difficult) was spending a long time drawing the fine details of Romeo's face. He suggested she didn't spend too long drawing pictures because she would have to finish it for homework and she could do illustrations at home. She should complete the main details in class while she had the text. She concurred and, at least while he was standing next to her, took her biro and started to print a few words neatly above the arrow she'd drawn from her pencil line.

A few tables behind Samantha, Julie wanted to know whether they had to do quotes for each entry and he suggested she should try to, pointing out that the words they could use were in the book and one of the 'lesson objectives' was to 'identify key quotes from the text'. Hilary wanted to know if she could go to the toilet and he reminded her of the rules. She pointed out that it could be a 'women's thing' and he conceded the point, but at the end of the day, rules are rules.

He walked down the neighbouring aisle, pleased that his day was proceeding without fuss, bother or likely hindrance. At the back of the class, Candy was finishing her one or two words from the balcony scene and looked up as he drew close to her desk.

'Is that okay sir?' she asked, raising both eye and exercise book toward him for confirmation that she was doing it right. So many of them it seemed these days, sought confirmation that they were 'doing it right'; he wished they'd be a little more independent, but it wasn't easy.

He glanced down at the neatly drawn icons and words carefully copied from the book and underlined in pencil. It looked fine.

'That's fine Candy,' he said.

'Thankyou sir,' she replied, her desire for approval satisfied at least for the moment. He was about to turn his attention to the next row when she sought his attention again.

'Sir.' She placed her ruler on her paper and looked up as he turned again to face her. She was looking out of the window now and when he was near enough, she pointed at a house just beyond the tennis court.

'Sir, that's my house there. Third one from the end with the red curtains.'

There was an air of triumph at a disclosure that probably wasn't public knowledge; a private little snippet, just between the two of them. He followed the line of her finger to one of the semi-detached houses maybe sixty or seventy yards away. The house was typical of the area's pleasant 'leafy suburb'- type semi's, complete with white-washed walls, interwoven vines climbing the walls and a rear garden complete with greenhouse and what looked like an apple or a pear tree at the far end.

'That's my room there,' she continued, still pointing with her forefinger. 'The one on the right with the red curtains, with the drain pipe going down the wall just on the left. Can you see?'

He leaned down slightly over her desk to follow the line of her pointing.

'Yes, I see. Looks like a nice little room. Doesn't take you long to get to school does it?'

She smiled at the customary observation made when people heard how close she lived to the school.

'No sir.' She took her pen in her hand and was poised to continue writing when she stopped again. 'Sir, I see you every morning when you're doing things in the classroom, moving books and tidying up the shelves. How comes you get here so early sir?'

It was his turn to smile.

'I prefer to,' he said. 'I can get quite a lot done at that time of the morning. The school's nice and quiet and I like it like that.'

She nodded, seemingly satisfied with his explanation and turned to Tanya, her neighbour, to borrow her pink while she wasn't using it, to shade in her Romeo's face.

His day was routinely uneventful. He set his alarm for six o clock, ate a bowl of cereal whilst packing the few things he needed into a shoulder bag, in order to leave for school about six thirty. It took about twenty five minutes to drive to school and on arrival, the first priority was a cup of tea. The kettle stood on the radiator shelf in his classroom and as the water boiled, he'd tidy his desk, replace the pens from the previous day in the red or black pencil case, slot loose worksheets back into their wallets and sit down to plan the day's lessons. He'd always liked being at school at this hour when silence prevailed and the only evidence of other activity was the occasional clatter of a cleaner's bucket in a nearby corridor.

The next morning he arrived at the usual time, popped the tea bag in his mug, took the things he needed out of his bag and tidied his desk. He picked a few books off the trolley by the side and took them to the back of the room to the bookshelves where he kept the pupils' exercise books and the sets of text books currently in use.

Outside, dawn was beginning to surface and the sky was a rich inky blue, broken only by the silver ball of the moon hovering low over the distant roof tops. A slight breeze stirred the leaves of the giant elm tree outside his room just to the left of the tennis court.

Having replaced the books at the back of the room and returned to his desk, he realised that he'd forgotten two exercise books he needed to mark for first lesson. He went back to the shelf to retrieve them and as he checked on top of the pile for the ones he'd placed horizontally as a reminder, he took his usual glance out of the window.

Apart from a few morning lights dotting house fronts and the lines of yellow headlights passing monotonously beyond the school gate, there was little to see at such an early hour. Except, as he looked to the right beyond the corner of the tennis court, his eye was caught by a movement at one of the windows.

Only after a moment or so did he realise it was Candy's room, the one she'd pointed out during the lesson yesterday. There was a low lamplight in the room and a shadow moving around in it.

Seconds later, the shadow sharpened to a figure, half silhouetted, slightly to the right of the centre of the window, virtually in semi-profile. Even at this distance it was recognisable as Candy. Though he couldn't see her in full detail, it was definitely her. He could make out her features and the long flowing hair falling onto her shoulders.

She stood for a while and then slightly rearranged herself under the light. And then suddenly and quite out of the blue, she lifted her hands to the points of her shoulders and slowly started to remove the straps of her nightie down her arms. His eyes fell on her naked breasts. Although his vision was limited, he could see the dark-pointed swells in the bedside light as she stood still, maintaining her semi-profile pose, until she turned and stood statuesque for a moment and then raised her hand and waved, just a slight wave – like a Royal wave from the Queen's motorcade – before turning back into her room and disappearing from sight.

He quickly busied himself with books and anything else that that lay scattered on the shelf and then returned to his desk, stunned by the intrusion into his early morning routine. He sat in his chair and continued to move things; anything, at random, like chess pieces – pens, a stapler, a board wiper – anything he could find at hand, in an attempt to occupy himself.

He had done nothing wrong of course; s*he* had exposed herself and it was *she* who had waved. Directly, it was nothing to do with him. But she was a pupil…. A child? …Not in the literal sense of the word. It was, after all, a secondary school and she was at the more senior end of the age range.

He took his *teachers planner* from the pile of books on his desk to set about preparing his lessons as usual, resolved that when it was her lesson, lesson three, everything would be as normal. He would set the work and they would get on with it. He would neither ignore her, nor would he award her any undue attention.

As it transpired, it *was* just another lesson. She entered the room with her friends and with little more than a glance in his direction, took her seat and got on with her work like the rest of the class. Only with about five minutes to go, when she raised her hand to request his help and he stood a little self-consciously at her side, did she fleetingly meet his eyes with her own, wearing a slight smile. He returned the smile briefly and then looked away and made his way back to his desk.

The next day he entered his classroom at the usual time, flicked the switch on the kettle, emptied his bag of the things he needed and tidied his desk. When he was ready, he made his way down the aisle vaguely aware of the early morning darkness outside. He found one of the wallets he needed and turned to place it on the back table, turning himself in full vision from outside as he did so, but keeping his eye on the wallet. He then turned back to the shelf and lifted half a pile of exercise books.

He placed the books on the table and stopped.

He was facing the window and could see the branches of the elm tree swaying gently in the breeze and a few dotted lights in nearby houses and to the right, a clearer, starker rectangle of light in one of the upper windows.

He watched, as, for the second day running, Candy appeared in semi-profile pose, her hair cascading onto her shoulders. He saw her lift her hands to the strands of her nightie and slide them slowly off her shoulders and down her arms. And for the second day running, he found himself staring at her semi-illuminated form, soft and glowing under her bedside light. And then, just as she had done yesterday, she raised an arm and made a quick wave of her hand, and almost as a reflex action, he raised his hand and waved back.

Seconds later she turned and disappeared from sight and he turned and walked back to his desk, leaving the exercise books and wallets on the back table.

It was arguably the 'wave' that cemented things. He sat at his desk grappling with the stapler – that never worked because the staples always gathered to gnarl at their exit point – on the table top and gazed at the back wall. It hadn't been so startling as yesterday – except that now he was part of the 'game' – a willing participant.

Her lesson was the first after lunch and like yesterday, it passed with little communication between them. She worked sensibly, discussing *'the various courses of action open to Romeo and Juliet'* with Tanya and Nicole. And for his part, like yesterday, he neither deliberately ignored her, nor awarded her any undue attention. It was only towards the end of the lesson, at about the same point as yesterday, as he undertook a final tour-of-duty that she raised her hand and shifted her book in his direction. As he approached she looked up and for a moment their eyes met.

'Is that alright sir? Have I done it right?' She showed him the little spider diagram she had drawn.

'It looks fine Candy,' he said, drifting his eye over her shoulder to seek the distraction of Tanya's book at her side.

'Thankyou sir.'

The following morning he emptied his bag, cleared his desk and with the mug of tea at the ready, made his way once again to the back of the room to get the materials he'd need for two of the morning's lessons. He lifted a folder from the shelf and turned to place it on the rear table, pausing mid-turn in front of the window to count the worksheets to make sure there were enough. He placed a second wallet on top and then stopped and stared out at the branches of the elm tree, which – in the picture-book stillness of the dark morning – had a forbidding, gaunt look, like monsters in children's books.

He looked to the right where Candy was already standing at her window. With slightly less delay than on the previous two mornings, her hands rose to her shoulders and slipped the nightie straps down her arms. He watched her breasts come into view. She raised her hand and waved in his direction and he raised his hand and waved back.

And so it became their little ritual. Each and every morning, they would take their places, and for a few private moments there they would remain, staring and waving across the wintry darkness into the lamplight of each others' room, until, with a final wave, she would move away from the window and he would return to his desk to set about preparing his lessons.

In class they read the remaining scenes of the play, with Candy volunteering to read the part of Juliet. There was little communication between them except for occasional questions about the text and confirmation towards the end of the lesson that she had been 'doing it right' at which point their eyes would meet and maybe the briefest of smiles would pass between them before he averted his gaze to outside, where the elm tree stood still and stark in the wintry sunlight.

She too liked to look outside. It was a beautiful tree, and on a crisp winter's day the huge expanse of leaves seemed to hover like the wings of a tiny aircraft, saturated in a rich and luxuriant green. She loved to stare at it from her bedroom window, particularly at night when its haunting flanks heaved and floated, as if waving gently into the neighbouring homes – the tips of the branches shining like the wing-tips of giant ghosts.

It was a few weeks later, an hour or so into the day that, in response to a memo, he knocked on the Headmistress's door and waited. He was ushered in and took his place in the armchair in front of her desk. She was a thin-lipped, slightly forbidding woman, who, maybe wisely, made a point of maintaining a distance – both from the pupils and in her dealings with staff. She looked him in the eye and spoke simply and unequivocally.

A matter had been brought to her notice involving him and a pupil. He had been observed in what could only be described as, an 'uncompromising situation'. She made the position clear, both from a personal perspective and from her position as the Head of the school – in that the welfare and well-being of the girls were her prior responsibility. She asked if he had anything to say. He mumbled a few apologetic words confirming there had never been any question of anything going on between them. She pointed out that that wasn't necessarily the point – he was a teacher, and teachers are placed in a position of trust.

Finally, she stood and handed him a brown manila envelope and informed him that he must leave the premises immediately.

He made his way round by the dining hall to his car.

He opened the door and took his place behind the steering wheel. He took the long brown envelope from his pocket and withdrew the folded A4 paper. The school's emblem and coat of arms were emblazoned across the top. The letter simply clarified the position. He read down the lines:

> ...*inappropriate conduct......a minor.....abuse of position...*

And the conclusion:

> ...*suspension from duties to take immediate effect, pending permanent dismissal......*

He folded the paper and replaced it in the envelope which he then placed in his pocket. He started the engine. As he drew the car round the corner into the drive he glanced up at Candy's window.

There was no sign of life at this time of day. The curtains were partly drawn and there was an empty darkness between them. He turned his attention back to the drive and drove past the huge branches of the elm tree to the main road, where he turned left to make his way home.